I0636099

Chasing the Dragon

By David E York

COPYRIGHT PAGE

Chasing the Dragon© [2025] [David York]

All rights reserved.

No part of this publication may be reproduced, distributed, or transmitted in any form or by any means, including photocopying, recording, or other electronic or mechanical methods, without the prior written permission of the author, except in the case of brief quotations embodied in critical reviews and certain other noncommercial uses permitted by copyright law.

This is a work of fiction. Names, characters, places, events, and incidents are either the product of the author's imagination or used in a fictitious manner. Any resemblance to actual persons, living or dead, events, or locales is purely coincidental.

Some real companies, products, and brand names are mentioned in this book for the sake of realism. All product names, logos, brands, and trademarks are the property of their respective owners. Their use in this work of fiction is solely for descriptive or identification purposes and does not imply any affiliation with or endorsement by those companies.

Cover design by [100covers.com]
Edited by [Kayla Wilkinson]

TABLE OF CONTENTS

Prologue

The buzzing needle filled the dim studio with a low, angry hum. Sam Logan sat still, her arm extended across the leather rest, palm down, eyes fixed on the curling image forming on her skin. It was a dragon. Not the fire-breathing, Western kind with wings and claws, but something older. Sleek, serpentine. Native, maybe. The head coiled back over the shoulder in an almost protective stance. She had picked it from a wall of flash art months ago and hadn't stopped thinking about it since.

"Looks good on you," the tattoo artist mumbled through his mask, focused on the shading around the eye. Sam didn't answer. The pain was a welcome distraction, clean, sharp, and real. Better than the vague emptiness that had been following her lately, like a shadow she couldn't shake. She'd been tired for weeks. Not the kind of tired that sleep could fix, but a bone-deep heaviness that clung to her no matter how many cups of coffee she drank or how many late-night tattoo sessions back at the shop she had.

1

It would be months before the dreams started. Before the voice in the dark whispered her forgotten name. Before the truth about what happened to her family clawed its way up from beneath the floorboards of her mind. But the dragon would be there, waiting, etched in ink and instinct, watching over her like it always had.

She just didn't know it yet.

Chapter 1 - The Reinvented Life

The needle hummed like a trapped wasp as Sam dragged ink across a stranger's skin, steady hand, blank mind, just the way she liked it. In the shop's low buzz and fluorescent hum, she could almost forget the gaps in her memory, the childhood tragedy no one talked about, the name Rebekka that sometimes echoed in dreams like a whisper meant for someone else. Outside, Fresno steamed in the late afternoon heat, but in here, surrounded by ink and antiseptic and the low thrum of Julie's music in the back room, Sam was safe, until the dragon started waking up.

Sam, real name Rebekka, lost her family in an accident. Or at least, that's what she had been told.

She was nine years old when it all happened. Her little brother Jason was five. She missed him most of all: him, their mom, and their dad. But Sam had no memory of what happened, just what others told her. The story always came packaged in the same hushed voices and half-sincere frowns: tragic accident, no survivors except her, lucky to be alive.

She never felt lucky.

She had never met her mother's family. She vaguely remembered something about how they disowned her for running off with Sam's father. Her father had several siblings, but none were willing to take her in after the accident. And her grandparents, on her father's side, wanted nothing to do with her. Sam had no idea why. All she knew was that one minute she had a family, and the next she was sitting on a couch in a stranger's house, clutching a stuffed bear that didn't smell like home.

She was an outcast in her own bloodline.

Foster care followed. So did the therapy. They gave her pills. Told her she was coping "remarkably well." But Sam wasn't coping. She was surviving.

Now twenty-seven, Sam lived a different life. A better one. She was confident, independent, and a damn good tattoo artist. She co-owned *Dragon Tattoo and Piercings* in Fresno, California, far from the childhood town she never revisited, and far from anyone who might call her Rebekka.

Jason used to call her "Sam" when he was little. No one really knew why, but the nickname stuck.

She kept it after everything, as if clinging to that name might keep some piece of him alive.

Sam didn't do relationships. "I don't have time for that nonsense," she'd say whenever someone asked. A few friends drifted in and out of her life, but only Julie stayed. Julie was her ride-or-die. They met at a tattoo convention in Anaheim, hit it off instantly, and within six months were running a shop together. Sam may not believe in soulmates, but if she did, Julie would be a contender.

She remembered the day they met like it was yesterday. Sam had been walking the crowded exhibit hall when she overheard a scuffle, not a conversation, more like an argument. A guy who looked like a Hell's Angels reject was harassing a petite blonde, tossing out sleazy remarks and trying to *"touch"* the tattoos on her legs. No security in sight, not unusual at events like this, so Sam decided she wasn't going to just walk past and let it slide.

She stepped in, wedged herself between them, and told the guy to try his *"handy work"* on her, if he dared. He dared.

Needless to say, he needed to be helped out of the convention to find his balls. After that, she and Julie were thick as thieves.

The foster homes she was in and out of always had the answer to her problems. At the request of the foster system and her case worker, the foster parents were told to take her to psychiatrists to work out her issues and perhaps be given something to help her. She had been visiting psychiatrists' offices and pharmacies ever since then.

The psychiatrists never helped. Sam still didn't remember the accident, nothing from the month before, or the month after. Not even the funerals. The memory loss baffled everyone, including herself. It wasn't like she was a baby at the time. She could remember some things. But the rest was just... black.

The pills made things worse. Antidepressants, sleeping meds, anxiety cocktails, at some point, she stopped keeping track. There were nights she'd knock out and not wake up for two or three days straight. Once, she nearly slipped into a coma. Julie found her and got her to the ER just in time. They said she was lucky.

That word again. Lucky.

But the strangest part, the part no one could explain, was the dreaming, or lack of it. Eighteen years. Not a single dream. Not even the fuzzy kind you forget by breakfast. Just darkness every time she closed her eyes.

Some said it was trauma. Others blamed the meds. Some doctors believed it was just how her brain rewired itself after the accident.

Sam didn't care anymore. She was used to the silence. Besides, it gave her more hours in the night. While others slept, she sketched. Dozens of her designs had been featured in tattoo magazines. She'd even been interviewed for *Ink Masters* once, but she turned it down.

"I don't need that kind of headache or critique in my life," she said.

She didn't chase fame. She didn't chase love.

But sometimes, late at night, she still chased something else.

The truth.

The dragon.

The visions started after a rough patch.

Sam was closing the shop late one night. Julie had already left to meet her boyfriend Ronnie, for a few drinks. Sam told her not to worry about it; she could close by herself.

"Thanks, Mommy, I can do it. I'm a big girl now," she'd said, grinning. They both laughed.

Sam swept the floor and tidied up, prepping the shop for the next day. She didn't realize she'd forgotten to lock the front door. That was usually Julie's job.

A man walked in.

He looked normal enough, just another customer wanting to browse the fresh designs on the wall. Sam was caught off guard, but kept her cool.

"Hey, I'm sorry, guy, but we're closed for the night," she said. "I forgot to lock up and flip the sign. Tell you what, come back in the morning, and if you see something you like, I'll knock ten percent off. Sound good?"

The man didn't answer.

8

He looked up from the book of sketches and punched Sam so hard she blacked out. A few of her teeth broke on impact.

From the bruises on her face, the cracked ribs, and torn ligaments in her arms, the doctors said he must have kicked and beaten her long after she hit the floor. But he never said a word. Just walked in, beat the hell out of her, and left. He didn't steal anything. Didn't even mess up the place.

The security camera caught it all. Sam gave the footage to the cops. They haven't caught him yet.

But if Sam ever saw him again, she wouldn't hesitate, she'd put him in the ground without a second thought.

She tried to move on, but something inside her had broken. She didn't tell Julie how bad it was, but fear settled into her bones. She started leaving the shop early, coming up with excuses not to come in at all. Julie didn't press her, she knew what was happening. Sam was struggling, and Julie was scared that if she pushed too hard, Sam would leave. And Julie couldn't imagine the shop, or her life, without Sam.

9

Then came the night Sam didn't wake up.

A month after the attack, still on pain meds and antibiotics, Sam took a bottle of sleeping pills and half her depression meds. She collapsed into a coma on the living room floor.

Julie didn't find her for nearly a full day. She'd tried calling over and over, but only got voicemail, until the phone died completely. The line went cold: "This number is no longer in service."

That's when Julie panicked.

She closed the shop, on a busy Friday, no less, and drove to Sam's apartment. She had a spare key, so she let herself in.

What she found haunted her.

Sam was face down on the floor, unconscious but somehow still breathing. Her eyes were open. Wide open. But Sam wasn't there; she was just gone.

The doctors said she'd slipped into a deep coma, but no one could explain how she survived the dosage.

Inside, Sam was nowhere. Blackness, as always. No sound, no movement. But then, something stirred.

A voice.

Rough, like gravel under metal. **"I've been waiting for you, Rebekka. It's been such a long time."**

The voice echoed all around her. Cold. Familiar.

"I've been watching you for eighteen years," it said. "I'm glad you finally decided to come back. I was starting to think you'd forgotten about me. And I thought we were such good friends."

"Who... who are you?" Sam whispered.

"Oh no... you've *forgotten*?" it laughed. Deep. Bone-chilling. Like something old and rotted was laughing through broken teeth.

"I'll let you try and remember, Rebekka. But I'll help you along."

There was a pause. A smile behind the darkness.

"Say, how's your family, Rebekka? And your tasty little brother... what was his name again... Jason?"

Another long, terrible laugh.

11

Sam's eyes flew open.

"Nurse! She's awake! Get the doctor, she's awake! Thank the Lord, she's awake!" Julie shouted, rushing back and forth from the door to the bed, tears running down her cheeks.

"Sam, Sam, you're awake! Thank goodness, you're awake…"

Julie was sitting on the edge of the bed, holding Sam's hand tightly. Her voice cracked with relief. "How do you feel? You had us scared for a bit, you've been in a coma for a week."

The doctor finally entered the room and stepped to Sam's side, beginning his evaluation. He checked her eyes, pulse, heart, the usual, but also ran a small monitor over her temple to read brain activity and oxygen levels.

"Ms. Logan, how do you feel? Any numbness? Spots in your vision?" he asked while gently pressing his stethoscope to her chest.

Before Sam could answer, another figure stepped into the room. An older woman, sharp-looking, professionally dressed, holding a small leather-bound notebook. She wore a name tag:

Dr. Rachel West, Psychiatrist.

Dr. West stood quietly near the door, waiting respectfully while the physician completed his exam. Julie noticed her first. She turned sharply toward the doorway.

"What the hell is *she* doing here?" Julie hissed, her voice low but venomous. "Haven't your kind done enough to Sam already? Doctor," she snapped, turning toward him. "Can't you do something? Sam doesn't need *her* here."

The doctor paused and looked between Sam and Julie. "I'm sorry," he said with a sigh. "It's protocol. Anytime someone overdoses, the hospital is legally required to notify the on-call psychiatrist. Dr. West is good. I assure you, she won't push Sam beyond what the law requires."

He finished checking the last of Sam's vitals and gave her a small, concerned smile. "You appear to be recovering well, Ms. Logan. You're very lucky. The amount of medication in your system should have ended your life. Frankly, I can't even explain how you came out of the coma."

He turned to leave. "I'll check on you again this evening. Thank you, Doctor," Julie said, her tone softening slightly as he exited.

He glanced at Dr. West as he passed her. She nodded once without saying a word.

"Hello, Ms. Logan," Dr. West said gently, stepping closer. "I'm Dr. Rachel West. I've been asked to speak with you to assess your state of mind, to make sure you're no longer at risk of harming yourself."

Sam looked over at Julie, her voice dry. "It's okay. I'll be fine. Not like I can get out of bed anyway." She motioned toward the soft restraints on her right arm and both legs. "Go get yourself some coffee. Maybe a muffin. Please." Julie hesitated. Her eyes bounced between Sam and Dr. West. "I'll be right down the hall," she said finally. "Call the nurse if you need me." She gave Dr. West one last dirty look before slipping out of the room.

Dr. West moved to the chair beside Sam's bed. "Would it be alright if I called you Rebekka?"

"No," Sam replied firmly. "Not Rebekka. You can call me Sam. Don't ask why, it takes too long to explain." She reached for the remote to raise the head of the bed, flinching as her ribs pulled tight and her arm ached. Bruises and broken bones, still healing from the beating.

"That's fine. Sam, then," Dr. West said, nodding. "Are you still feeling suicidal? Any desire to hurt yourself?"

"No," Sam said quietly. "Not anymore. I'm okay. But please... no more pills. I don't want any more pills."

"I understand," Dr. West said. "And I agree. No more medications for now, at least not until you're stronger. But now, the hard question: Why did you try to end your life, Sam? Whatever you're going through, there's always a way through it. Everything can be overcome, with help, or sometimes, yes, even alone."

Sam hesitated, then looked over at the psychiatrist. "Do you have a file on me? Did the hospital give you my background?"

"I have a little," Dr. West replied. "The incident at your shop, your high usage of sleeping pills and antidepressants. That's about it."

She gave Sam a look of gentle curiosity. "I'm here to understand if you're still in the same frame of mind you were when this happened. That's all."

Sam tried to get more comfortable, but the restraints kept her from moving much. "Dr. West, I'll be happy to answer your questions, but can you do anything about these?" she asked, motioning toward the restraints.

"I'll have the nurse remove the arm restraint," Dr. West replied. "But the ankle restraints have to remain in place for twenty-four hours. Again, it's state law."

She stepped to the doorway and called out to the nurse's station. A few moments later, a nurse entered the room, unfastened the wrist restraint, and then exited quietly.

Dr. West returned to the chair beside Sam's bed. "So, Sam," she asked gently, "what was so bad that you felt ending your life was the only option?"

Sam shifted as much as the restraints allowed. She adjusted the oxygen line beneath her nose, then looked down at her hands. "Dr. West, I've been pretty independent, really, for most of my life. No one ever gave a crap about me. Julie and I opened the shop, and we've been very successful. I've never been afraid of anyone... but after the beating I took, I couldn't get it out of my mind. It kept looping, over and over again." She paused, searching for the right words.

"I could sleep just fine, well, I mean, I don't dream, so that wasn't an issue. It was when I was awake... I couldn't stop thinking about it. What could have happened? What I did to provoke it. If I did anything at all."

Her voice dropped.

"It scared me. Even to the point that I wanted to bail on Julie and leave the shop. I guess it just got so bad that I couldn't shake it, and I didn't want to

17

be a drag on her. So, I figured I'd just... slip off to sleep and not wake up."

Just then, something flickered behind her eyes, a quick flash. A whisper from the dark.

"I' ve been waiting for you."

Sam blinked.

"Sam?" Dr. West leaned in slightly. "Are you okay? You looked like you just remembered something. Was it the attack?"

Sam shook her head slowly, her brows furrowed. "No... no... I don't think so. I... I had a memory. Or something like one. I don't know what it was. Guess it wasn't anything."

Dr. West didn't press. "That's fine. Is it safe to say you won't be doing that again? Hurting yourself, I mean?"

Sam took a breath. "No. I think I'll be fine. I just... I don't know how to get over this fear that something like that attack could happen again."

"That's a very real and logical fear, Sam. It's understandable. But you can't let it control you, your actions, your thoughts, your future. The man who attacked you... He may have been targeting

18

you, but he also may have been high, or mentally ill, or reacting to something that had nothing to do with you."

Dr. West paused. "Did they ever catch him?"

Sam looked over at the muted TV, then toward the window. "No. Not yet. Even with the video I gave the cops, they haven't found him."

She turned back to Dr. West. "But you're right. I need to put it behind me. I need to get back to my old self. It might take time... but I think I can do it."

"That sounds like a solid plan, Sam. Don't rush it. Take it slow. Small steps lead to big accomplishments. And if you ever need someone to talk to, about anything, you can call me. No charges, no appointments. It's on me. I just want to see you recover."

Dr. West closed her leather notebook and set it in her lap. "I can see you're a strong woman, Sam. I can also see that, at some point, you've had a hard life. I'll leave my card on your table. You will get through this."

"Thank you, Dr. West. I will. And I'll call if I start feeling the stress, or if that fear starts creeping in again."

Dr. West stood, walked toward the door, then paused and turned.

"Remember, you can overcome those thoughts."

With that, she opened the door and stepped out into the hallway, leaving Sam alone with her thoughts.

Sam looked up and shut off the TV. She rarely watched it anyway, always considered it a brain drain. When the screen went black, her reflection appeared in the glass. But she wasn't alone. There was something in the room.

In the corner, just a black shape. No form, no features. Like smoke in a mirror. A shadow with no source. Sam turned quickly, eyes locked on the corner.

Empty.

She looked back at the TV. Just her reflection now.

Chapter 2 - Bumpy Road to Recovery

"So, you were worried about me having the shop?" Julie's voice broke the silence as she walked in, trying to lighten the mood. "Listen to me, Sam, if you ever pull that crap again, you won't have to do yourself in. I'll do it for you."

Julie gave a crooked smile, trying to mask the weight of her words. "I can run the shop without you. But I can't do *life* without my partner in crime."

Another smile, and this time, a tear rolled down her cheek.

"I was so scared you weren't coming back," she said softly. "This wasn't like the last time. The doctors… they'd pretty much written you off. No brain waves. They listed you as vegetative."

Julie walked to the bed and leaned in, touching her forehead to Sam's.

"Ride or die, baby. Ride or die."

Sam gave her a weak hug as best she could, wrapping one arm around Julie's shoulders. "I'm sorry. I'm so sorry you had to find me like that. I promise you, here and now, I won't ever do that to you again."

Two weeks later, Sam was back at the shop.

She started slow, scheduling sessions, helping Julie close, keeping close to the front of the shop. It was hard at first. The fear didn't vanish overnight. But Julie never pressured her, never rushed her. She just stood beside her, steady and solid. That strength made all the difference.

One evening, Sam's newest client came in for his first session. They were starting the outline for a new tattoo, a dragon. Dark, twisted, evil-looking. Its body coiled from his shoulder down to his hand, curling in tight spirals around the bone and muscle.

The dragon's eyes, deep and shadowed, would glow red when finished. The design was intense. Sam loved it.

She leaned in and started outlining the face, needle buzzing steadily in her hand.

Then it hit.

"It's been such a long time…" A voice. Deep. Cold. Familiar. And the eyes, glowing red in the dark. Not ink. Not skin. Something *else*.

Sam jerked back on her stool, chest tightening.

"Hey, you okay?" the client asked, turning his head slightly.

"What? Yeah... yeah, I'm okay. Just a cramp in my hand. Give me a sec, gonna grab some water." She stood and walked quickly to the back, slipping past the heavy curtain divider.

Julie glanced up from her own station, mid-session with a client. She saw the look on Sam's face, but didn't say a word. Just nodded slightly and gave her space. She'd call if she was needed.

Sam leaned against the wall behind the curtain. The voice. The eyes. Something in the flash was trying to push through. A buried memory. No, a presence. It wasn't just *inside* her head. It was waiting. Watching. Forcing itself back into her life.

She crossed to the mini fridge, pulled out a water, and took a long sip. Then she returned to her station.

"Sorry, my mouth was getting dry," she said, settling back into her seat. "Let's finish the outline, and then we'll set a day for color. This is gonna be a really bad-ass tat. Could be one of the best dragons I've done."

"Sweet," said the client, grinning. "Can't wait to see it done."

***

The next few days flew by.

Staying busy helped Sam stay focused. Occupied. It dulled the thoughts and quieted the worries, at least for a while.

On Tuesday, a slow day at the shop, Sam, Julie, and Ronnie closed early and headed down the street to *The Eye Patch*, their favorite local pub. It was a dimly lit little place with pool tables, strong drinks, and regulars who minded their own business.

"You're really good, Sam," Ronnie said, taking a sip from his whiskey shot. "Your dragons? Some of the best I've ever seen. I totally get why you were featured in *Ink Magazine*."

He shot a look over at Julie, realizing too late what he'd said. She frowned and shook her head slightly. "I mean, uh, almost as good as Julie's. Hers are rock solid," he added. Julie smirked and gave Sam a playful shove on the shoulder.

Julie looked over at Sam, "Please. I can't even be in the same room when it comes to dragons compared to Sam. She's probably the best dragon tattoo artist alive." Julie leaned forward, proud. "She didn't even apply for *Ink Master* that year, they came to *her*. That says everything."

Ronnie nodded, then grinned. "Now if we could just get her a date..." Julie quickly elbowed him.

Sam raised an eyebrow but didn't look bothered. Julie knew better, Sam wasn't interested in dating. She was wired differently. Some people were just meant to be solo, and that was Sam. Julie had learned to respect that.

"Sorry," Ronnie said, holding up his hands. "Didn't mean to be the wet sock on our first outing in forever."

"No harm, Ronnie. I know you're just looking out for me," Sam said with a small smile. "You and Julie are plenty for me. I don't need anybody else."

She lifted her glass.

"To the trio."

"To the trio," Julie and Ronnie echoed, and they clinked glasses.

The drinks were cold. The air warm. And, for a moment, it felt like everything was okay again, normal.

The trio left the pub, Julie and Ronnie heading back to Julie's place, and Sam walking home to her apartment alone. It was dark and quiet, just the way Sam liked it.

She locked the door behind her and slipped off her boots. For the first time in a long time, she felt tired. Maybe she'd actually sleep tonight. The real kind of sleep, not just lying down for four hours with nothing but silence in her head.

She passed by her drawing desk, reached over, and clicked on the lamp. The soft pool of light spilled across her scattered sketches. She glanced down and smirked.

"I think I'm getting better," she muttered. "My drawings look better, more controlled... more detailed." She turned to head to the bathroom, and almost stumbled backward.

There, in the shadows cast by the desk lamp, stood the same smokey silhouette she'd seen in the hospital. No form. No face. Just dark, swirling nothingness, like a burnt reflection trying to take shape.

Sam gasped, lunged toward the lamp, and switched it off.

She turned back to the bathroom.

Nothing there now. Just the faint glow of the nightlight plugin reflecting in the mirror.

"Take a breath, girl. In through the nose, out through the mouth," she whispered to herself. "You're just tired. That's all. Just a weird shadow from the lamp."

She walked to the bathroom, got ready for bed, and then headed down the hall to her room. She plugged her phone into the charger, slid under the sheet, and, for the first time in years, fell into a deep sleep.

Chapter 3 - Dreams & Visions

This time…the first time in eighteen years… she dreamed.

Sam stood alone in darkness. No light. No sound. Just stillness. Then, behind her, a light blinked on, her drawing table, lit up exactly as it looked at the shop. Paper ready. Drawing pencils laid out. A full set of colors nearby.

She walked over and picked up a pencil.

At first, she didn't know what she was drawing. Her hand moved, but she wasn't guiding it. Something else was. She watched as it sketched. Drew. Shaded. The lines came faster, more confident, more vivid, until finally, her hand dropped to her side. There, on the page, was a dragon. But not just any dragon. It wasn't one of her tattoo designs. It wasn't cartoonish or traditional or even like the one she'd started on her new client. This one was dark. Sinister. It had glowing red eyes, but not dragon eyes. *Human* eyes.

Its body was reptilian, scaly, monstrous… but it stood upright, like a man. Its face was almost beautiful, almost human, but twisted somehow. Wrong. Its gaze was powerful, and its presence overwhelming. She felt herself trembling even as she stared at her own lines on the page.

And then the voice came. "Hello, *Rebekka*. Nice of you to join me… here in my home."

A chill ran through her spine. The room around her was still black, except for the glowing light above the desk.

"I thought perhaps you weren't coming back," the voice continued. "Not after your… what was it again? Ah, yes, your little *attempt* to leave me. That's something we can't allow now can we?"

She spun around. Nothing there.

The voice was coming from the drawing.

"Yes, that's right, Rebekka. We are… very familiar with each other. You just need reminding."

Her breath caught. She looked back at the paper. The dragon's red eyes *followed her*, tracking her every move as she paced the darkness.

"Rebekka," it whispered. "How's the family? Mmm… what about your *tasty* little brother… what was his name again?" A cruel laugh echoed in the room.

"You don't get to talk about my family, *and not about Jason!*" Sam shouted, trembling.

"Ahh, yes. *Jason.* Thank you for reminding me..." The voice grew deeper, darker.

"We were meant for each other, Rebekka. Just like before."

Sam lunged at the table and tore the drawing into pieces, smashing the desk with both hands. The lamp burst into darkness, and everything went black again. Then, floating in the void, two *enormous* glowing red eyes opened. Watching her.

Sam jolted upright in bed, drenched in sweat. She couldn't remember the dream, but she remembered *dreaming*.

"That's the first dream I've had in eighteen years," she whispered, staring at the ceiling. "I wish I knew if it was a good dream or a bad one..." She already knew the answer. The *weight* of it told her. It was bad. She looked at the time. "Crap, 10:30?" she muttered. "I'm supposed to be at the shop at 11." She grabbed her phone and dialed. "Julie, hey, sorry. I'm running late this morning. I… I overslept, I guess," Sam said with a small laugh.

"Are you sure you're okay?" Julie asked on the other end, her voice tight with concern. "Do you need the day off?" Sam quickly replied, "No, I'm fine. I swear. All good. I'll be there in a bit."

"Okay. But if anything changes, let me know. No pressure." Julie's voice was full of concern.

"Sure thing, Mom," Sam teased gently.

She ended the call and sat on the edge of her bed, still catching her breath. Her fingers twitched. She remembered drawing something. But what? Sam made it to the shop just as her client walked in the front door.

She caught sight of the young woman settling into the lobby area. "I'll be right with you, Lucy. Just getting everything ready. I'll come grab you in five." With that, Sam disappeared through the back curtain.

"You good, girl?" Julie asked as Sam came through, tying her apron. "Yup, you know it! Let's rock!" Sam said, grabbing her tools and heading toward her station.

"Let's get takeout from Jei Lo for lunch, I'm starving," she called out over her shoulder, grinning.

Then she stepped into her work area… and froze. Her tools slipped from her hands, clattering loudly to the floor. Sam didn't move. Couldn't. She stared at her drawing table, her mind struggling to process what she was seeing.

There, sitting right next to the client's tattoo stencil, was another drawing. It was her family. Her mom, her dad, little Jason… and her. But it wasn't just a sketch. It was like a *nightmarish* family portrait.

Her face was *twisted*, distorted, her eyes glowing red, like the dragon in her client's tattoo. The others looked normal. But her… she looked like something else entirely. Like she didn't belong with them.

"Julie… who did this?" Sam's voice cracked. "Julie!"

Julie came running from the back. "What is it, Sam? What happened?"

"This isn't funny. Not funny at all. Did *you* do this? Who did this?"

Julie's eyes moved to the drawing table, brows knit in confusion. "Sam, that's the stencil for your client today. *You* did it. You've been working on it for the last three days. I thought you were happy with it?"

Sam blinked. Looked down at the table again. The nightmarish family sketch was gone. Only the stencil remained. Just the simple dragon outline for Lucy's tattoo. Nothing more.

"Where did it go? Julie, where, did you move it? The other drawing… where…?"

"Sam, honey," Julie said gently, reaching out to rub her back, "There isn't another drawing. That's all that's been on your table for three days. That's all you've been focused on."

"*No, dang it!*" Sam jerked away from Julie's hand. "Stop with the mom bit. Don't treat me like I'm your child!" Julie flinched and stepped back, stunned.

"There was *something* there! I saw it, my family… me, it was right there!"

34

Julie took another step back, arms slowly folding across her chest. "O... okay, Sam. I didn't mean anything by it. I'm just trying to help. I swear, there was nothing else on your table."

She turned away, walking quietly back to her station. Her client watched with wide eyes, concerned. Julie offered a small, apologetic smile.

"It's okay," she said to the client, trying to steer attention away from the tension. "She's just having a trying day. Happens to all of us. Let's take a look at some of these other designs."

Lucy, still sitting in the waiting area, leaned forward. "Is she still gonna do my tat today? I can come back if she needs time. It's really no rush."

Julie glanced over her shoulder at the curtain, concern deep in her eyes, but forced a reassuring smile. "No, no, she'll be out shortly. She's good."

Sam bent over, picking up her tools, but her eyes stayed fixed on the table. She slowly placed the tools back in the tray, then turned and walked to the back. Quietly. Purposefully.

She stepped into the bathroom and locked the door behind her. For a moment, she just stood there, staring at herself in the mirror. "What's wrong with you?" she whispered.

Maybe I hallucinated it. Julie didn't see anything. Just me.

She reached into her pocket and pulled out a bottle of pills. She held them in her palm and stared down at them, unmoving. She closed her eyes.

Suddenly, she saw faces, *her* family. Her mother, her father, Jason. They were in a car, somewhere on a trip. She didn't know where, but they were laughing, happy. Jason had his mouth open wide like he was mid-joke. Her mom was singing. Her dad was looking at her through the rearview mirror. Then it was gone.

Sam opened her eyes, looked at her reflection again, and back down at the pills. Finally, she put them back in her pocket. She turned on the sink, splashed her face with cold water, grabbed a towel, and dried off.

Then she unlocked the door and stepped out.

She walked to the lobby, where Lucy, her client, was still waiting patiently.

"You ready, Lucy?" Sam said, her voice steady now. "Let's do this. It's gonna be awesome. That design is gonna look amazing on your shoulder."

* * *

By the end of the day, the clients were gone. The shop quieted.

Julie was sweeping the shop floor in slow, even strokes. She hadn't said much to Sam since the episode earlier. She kept her head down, letting the broom glide across the tile.

Sam straightened her table. Checked it twice. No stray papers, no drawings that shouldn't be there. She walked out toward the front, double-checked the locks, and flipped the sign to *CLOSED*. Then she turned and walked up to Julie, who was still sweeping, still watching the ground.

Julie didn't look up. She *knew*, if she met Sam's eyes right now, she'd fall apart.

"Julie… Jules," Sam said, standing directly in front of her. Her voice soft, cracking. "Bestie. Please. Look at me."

Julie stopped sweeping. Sam already had tears falling from her eyes. Tiny taps hit the floor between them. Julie slowly looked up and locked eyes with her.

"You don't have to say it," Julie whispered. "I know. I know before you even say it, and I forgive you. I *accept* it." Julie stepped closer, voice trembling but strong. "You're my best friend. My *ride or die*. There's nothing you could do that would ever keep me from being your friend. *Nothing*. I care about you, girl. I just... I don't like seeing you like that. And I'm sorry if I sound like a mom sometimes. I just don't want to lose you, Sam. Do you understand?"

Sam nodded, holding back a sob.

"Julie... I could never, ever deserve a friend like you," she said. "But I have to say it. I'm sorry. *So* sorry for the way I spoke to you earlier. You didn't deserve that. You're the best thing in my life. You've been the best thing that's *ever* happened to me... since I lost my brother."

Sam paused, trying not to fall apart again. "I know you just want the best for me. And you don't want to see me... in a bad way." She avoided saying the s-word. Julie had seen the darkness in Sam, and never once ran from it.

Julie stuck with her, tighter than blood.

Sam stepped in. They hugged hard, tight, silent. Then Julie leaned back slightly and held out her fist. Sam smiled through her tears, returned the fist.

Bump.

Then they both cracked up.

"Bro, you good?" Sam asked in a deep mock voice. "Yeah, bro, I'm good," Julie answered, grinning. And the laughter carried them, just long enough, into the next moment.

Later that night, Sam climbed into bed. She didn't even bother turning off the bedside lamp, she was out cold within minutes.

The darkness returned. Darker than dark. Quiet. Still. Silent.

And then... the small light again. A soft glow. It bled into the void slowly until the shape of the *drawing table* emerged from it, just like before.

The dragon sketch was there. Whole. Untouched. *As if she had never torn it up.*

Its red eyes still glowed, glared, *tracked* her through the darkened dream space.

"Welcome back, Rebekka," the voice said. Smooth but hollow. "This is becoming quite the regular occurrence now, wouldn't you say? Just like old times."

The sketch was talking to her again. Sam took a step closer. "What is it you want from me? Who… or what… are you?"

"Oh, Rebekka… I'm hurt," came the deep, gravel-coated reply, followed by a sinister laugh that echoed like dragging chains. "We, you and I, are *very* familiar with one another. We go way back."

"I don't… I *can't* remember you."

A long, low growl of amusement shook the space around her.

"Did you enjoy my sketch?" the voice asked. "Such a *lovely* family, Rebekka. Your mother. Your father. And that tasty little brother of yours, Jason, yes? That *was* his name, wasn't it?"

Sam's chest tightened. "That drawing… that was *your* doing?"

Silence.

The room went black. The drawing table disappeared. The sketch vanished. And then the red, glowing eyes returned, closer now, larger. *Pulsing.* And behind them, below them, she could *almost* make out a form. A shape. A massive shadow in the smoke. *Alive.* Breathing. Watching.

"You're not quite there yet, Rebekka," it said. "But you're coming along... nicely."

It leaned in closer. The voice grew softer, more intimate, like an old friend or a predator.

"A few more helpful hints. A few more *reminders...* and then, you'll be ready. You'll remember who you really are. You'll be back to your old self."

A pause.

"I look forward to it," it whispered. "It'll be just like it used to be...
You and me, Rebekka."

Sam jolted awake, staring up at the ceiling. Her breath was ragged. Her sheets were damp with sweat. But she could *remember* something. More than before.

Red eyes.

A shape in the smoke.

And a dragon... that wasn't a dragon.

She sat up, her heart still pounding. "What does that mean?" she asked the empty room.

Sam went to work like any other day, sketching designs, talking with clients, laughing at Julie's dumb jokes. But the dream... it lingered. Bits and pieces floated in the back of her mind like flotsam from a shipwreck. Not enough to understand, just enough to distract. She felt like a walking zombie, functioning on the outside, but disconnected, wandering somewhere deep and silent inside.

And oddly, she was looking forward to sleep now. Looking forward to *the dream.*
Maybe it would reveal more. Maybe she could start putting together the pieces, like a jigsaw puzzle no one told her she owned.

After locking up the shop with Julie, Sam rushed home. She skipped dinner, got cleaned up, changed into her usual sleep tank and shorts, and climbed into bed.
Out cold within minutes.

Darkness again. But not like before.

No drawing table.

No red eyes.

No voice slick with venom and riddles.

Just... nothing.

Still. Empty. Quiet.

She stood there in that void, waiting. Searching. Nothing came.

She awoke with a start. Morning light pressed through her blinds. 7:03 a.m. She lay there, motionless, staring at the ceiling. Had there been a dream? She *felt* like there had. But it slipped through her mind like water through a cracked bowl. And then, A flash.

Her mom.

Jason.

Laying in a pool of blood.

Then, Nothing.

She sat up sharply in bed. Her heart kicked once, hard in her chest. *Was that a real memory?* Or just another fantasy manufactured by a broken brain hungry for answers? She felt tired, physically and mentally wrung out.

She got dressed, grabbed her bag, and left the apartment. A quiet craving pulled her to the local donut shop. She ordered a plain donut and a black coffee. Simple. No decisions. No emotions.

She got to the shop early. Too early. Julie wouldn't be in for another hour. Sam unlocked the door, flicked on the lights, and walked to her drawing table. She pulled out her sketches, nothing new. No red-eyed monstrosities. Just lines. Paper. Ink.

Still... the fog clung to her.

She reached into her pocket and felt the pill bottle. Just feeling it there made her exhale. Like it was a charm. A genie's bottle. A pressure valve. She didn't take one. Just touched it. Let it ground her.

The rest of the morning passed in a haze. She doodled. Sorted mail with Julie. Flipped through new tattoo books. Talked shop.

Then her next client walked in. The dragon client. The one with the sinister wraparound dragon she'd outlined over a week ago. The one with the glowing red eyes.

"You ready to do this?" Sam asked.

"Yes, ma'am. I've been stoked since the outline. Let's make this thing pop."

He laid down, arm outstretched. Sam prepped the colors, shading ink, line work black, and blood red for the eyes. Her tools were lined up in perfect order. Everything was normal.

They got started. His skin was perfect, no stretch, no resistance. Ink took like butter. No blowouts. Saturation was smooth and deep.

She was finishing the dragon's head now, detailing the eyes. A little more red. Maybe just a touch of shadow,

Then the dragon's eyes moved.

They tracked her. The pupils locked onto her face.

And from the inked mouth, a tongue, a *forked tongue*, seemed to *flick* at her cheek.

A voice slithered into her ear:

"Did you miss me, Rebekka?"

Sam *jerked back*, the needle gun slipping from her hand and clattering across the floor.

Her client craned his head back. "Whoa, you okay? Did your stool slide or something?"

But Sam didn't respond.

She couldn't. She was staring at the dragon. It was staring *back*.

"Julie, I, I've gotta go."

And with that, Sam bolted from the shop. She didn't wait for a response. Didn't even glance back.

Her client sat up from the table, still half-finished. "Uh… is someone gonna wipe this down and wrap it?"

Julie stood at the door, stunned. She didn't move until the chime above the door stopped echoing. "Yeah... yeah, I've got you," she said, walking back over. "Sorry about that. Give me a second."

The client glanced around, confused. "I think she just slipped off the stool? Maybe it rolled or something. I asked if she was okay, but... she didn't say a word."

Julie forced a smile, wiping down the fresh ink. "She'll be alright. Just a rough day."

Sam didn't go home. She walked aimlessly through the neighborhood, her head a mess. The memory of the dragon's eyes, of its tongue, of the *voice*, they looped in her head like a film reel on fire.

Eventually, she found herself at The Eye Patch. Familiar, dim, quiet.

She slid into a booth at the back and ordered two shots of whiskey. When they arrived, she slammed one down and stared at the second. Her hands cradled her face.

What the hell is happening to me?
Is this just leftover trauma from the OD? From years on and off pills?
Or am I cracking? Like, really cracking?

She reached into her pocket and pulled out the pill bottle. Set it on the table. Just stared at it.

Her phone buzzed, Julie's face lit up the screen. That same happy photo she'd used for years. Sam answered. "Hey, Julie. I'm fine, really." Julie's motherly tone of caution and concern, "I'm just checking in. Not gonna ask questions. If you wanna talk, I'm here. But no pressure."

47

Sam sighed. "Thanks. I… I don't know what to say yet. I don't know what even happened. But I *am* okay."

"Good. Just wanted to hear your voice. I'm really worried, Sam." Julie's voice cracked just a little.

"I'll try to be in tomorrow. If anything makes sense by then, I'll tell you." Sam said.

"Okay. Take care. Love you."

"Love you too."

She hung up and stared at the dark screen a moment longer. Then, with a sigh, she slid the pill bottle back into her pocket, finished her second shot, and left the pub.

* * *

Back home, she locked the door behind her and walked into the bathroom. She stared at her reflection. "Am I losing it?" she whispered. "Is this what a breakdown feels like?"

She washed her face and dried off, then changed into sleep clothes. Sitting on the edge of her bed, she looked at the sleeping pills on her nightstand.

"I just need sleep. *Real* sleep." She took one pill, swallowed it dry, and laid back under the sheets.

Darkness returned.

But this time, the shadows coiled tighter around her. And then, those red eyes. Larger than before. Burning brighter. The shape beneath them was clearer now. A humanoid figure, tall and thin. A face began to emerge, narrow, sharp, eerily beautiful.

"Hello again, Rebekka," the voice said. Smooth. Cutting. Dark silk.
"You were *so* rude to me today. That wasn't very nice."

Sam tried to move toward the shape, but her limbs were frozen.

"Your memories… they're coming back, aren't they?" the voice purred.
"You remember me yet?"

"I… I don't know you," she said.

A mocking laugh echoed. "You wound me, Rebekka. We've been *so* close. For so very long."

"Who are you? Why do you keep showing me these things? What do you want?"

49

The voice shifted, deepened, shook the walls around her:

"How would you prefer I speak to you? Like this?" Suddenly, the voice rang *inside her head*, vibrating her thoughts.

"Or this? Just like I have been?"

Then, a pause. "Or perhaps... another language?"

"No. English is fine," she said. "And... here. In this room. Whatever this is."

"Ah, so particular. You *have* changed, Rebekka."

The voice curled through her thoughts, like smoke and velvet.

"You'll remember soon," it said." It's all still there. You know things even the brightest minds could never dream of."

Another pause.

"Tell me... how is your family, Rebekka? Your father. Your sweet mother. And of course, Jason."

"Don't talk about them," she hissed. "I told you. They're off-limits."

"Oh Rebekka," the voice teased, "you *jest.*" The figure stepped back into the darkness. Only the glowing red eyes remained.

"We'll talk again soon. Try to be more... *hospitable* next time. Introduce me to your friends."

A grin spread through the smoke. And then, blackness.

Chapter 4 - Surf City

Sam jolted awake. Drenched in sweat. Sheets tangled around her. Her chest rose and fell like she'd run a marathon. She stared at the ceiling, heart racing.

She could still see them.

The red eyes.

The figure.

The voice.

Sam got up, showered, and left the apartment without even looking at her bed again. She swung by the donut shop and picked up a bacon and egg taco with a black coffee, then walked three blocks in the opposite direction of the shop, to the Surf City Internet Café. It was a dim little hole-in-the-wall joint that still smelled faintly of ashtrays and old carpet cleaner, but it was quiet and anonymous.

She paid for an hour of computer time and found a seat in the far back, against the wall where no one could see her screen. *Not using my phone. Not the shop's laptop. Julie's way too good with tech. She'd sniff my trail in five clicks.* The computer monitor flickered to life, sluggish but usable. She opened the Bravo browser and typed into the search bar:

"mythical two-legged dragons with red human eyes"

Click.

The little spinner spun and spun, the loading bar inching forward like it hated its job. "You'd think in this day and age it'd be faster," Sam muttered, sipping her coffee. "But what do I know?"

She took a bite of the taco, and her eyebrows lifted. "Holy cow! That's good! Or maybe I'm just starving."

Search results began trickling in, grainy images, old etchings, fantasy art, fan forums. A few thumbnails flashed across the screen, nothing yet that matched what she saw in the dream. She scrolled.

"Crap," Sam whispered. "I need to call Julie."

She pulled out her phone and tapped Julie's contact. The familiar photo of Julie smiling came up, cheeky, bright, alive. The line rang twice.

"Hey, Sam? Everything okay? What's wrong?" Julie's voice was sharp with concern.

Sam exhaled slowly, already feeling guilty. "Julie, calm down. Everything's fine. I just swung by the bookshop near my place. Wanted to check out some art books, maybe get inspired for new tattoo designs. Gotta keep the portfolio fresh, y'know?"

Lying sucks. Sam winced. *Especially to Julie. She's the best thing I've got.*

"I might drop by the donut shop before I head in. You want anything?"

Julie gave a disgusted laugh. "You *know* me. I had vegan eggs, plant-based bacon, and this new mushroom coffee that's actually pretty fire."

Sam gagged theatrically. "Bluhhh. I'm barfing over here."

Julie laughed. "Alright, nerd. See you in a bit."

"Later, Jules." Sam ended the call and slid the phone face down on the desk.

She turned back to the screen, now the results had expanded. More obscure images were trickling in, illustrations from ancient manuscripts, fourteenth-century carvings, medieval legends, and darker stuff, sketches of dragons linked to devils, fallen angels, dark dimensions, and end-of-days prophecies.

And then,

There it was.

She froze. One image on the third row: a two-legged creature, standing tall with a scaled torso, broad shoulders, a vaguely human head, but with sharp, alien features, and glowing red eyes. The background was ink-washed black. Its arms were outstretched like it was welcoming someone, or summoning them.

"What is that?" Sam whispered.

A man two tables over, looked up. "You talkin ' to me?"

Sam didn't even glance over. "No. Sorry."

Her eyes never left the image. Hand trembling slightly, she clicked the link beneath it.

The link led to a creature from Chinese mythology, something close, but still not quite right.

"Dang it," Sam muttered, leaning back in her chair.

Nothing matched. Why couldn't real life be like the movies? Open a browser, type three words, and everything you could ever need magically appears in one click. But no. Forty-five minutes of scrolling, clicking, cross-referencing, nothing came close. Nothing had the red, human eyes. Nothing had the ability to speak. Or vanish. Or crawl into your dreams like a parasite.

Maybe it doesn't exist, she thought. *Or maybe... I wasn't supposed to find it this way.*

With a frustrated sigh, Sam closed the browser, logged off, and shut down the monitor.

The screen went black. In the dim reflection of the glass, she saw herself, but something else too. Behind her. The smoke. The same black, hazy shape she'd seen in the hospital. In her apartment. And now here.

Only this time, there were *eyes* in the smoke, faint, glowing red. Sam spun around, and nearly slammed her face into the wall directly behind her. *What the hell?* She turned back to the screen. Just her reflection.

Then, a voice, low and calm, like silk laced with razors: "That's a futile effort, Rebekka."

Sam froze. Spun again. Left. Right. No one. She stormed toward the only other person in the room, a guy two seats over, scrolling through a forum with giant headphones around his neck.

"Hey," she snapped. "What did you just say to me?"

The guy looked up, blinking. "Are you mental or something? Only person talkin 'to the air in here is *you*."

He slid his headphones back on and shook his head, leaving Sam standing there, heart pounding, head spinning.

No one else was in the café. No music. No TV. No radios. But she'd heard it. Heard him. It was *the voice*. From the dream. She raised a hand to the back of her head and tugged her short black hair hard. "Ow," she muttered, flinching.

Not dreaming.

Sam grabbed her now-cold coffee and the last bite of the taco, dumped them both in the trash, and walked out into the heat and light of the street.

Her mind raced.

Is that you? she thought. *My dream... are you in my head now?*

No answer.

She cupped a hand near her mouth so no one would see. "Hey. I know it's you. You opened this dialogue. This is on you."

A beat of silence.

Then:

"A bit testy, aren't we, Rebekka?"

Her blood chilled.

"It would seem you're slowly coming around, my sweet girl."

"I'm *not* your girl," Sam snapped, loud enough this time that a man walking his dog gave her a sideways glance.

She looked down, muttered, "Hello? I'm talking to you." But there was no reply now. The voice was gone. It had sounded the same as in the dream, but now she was *awake*. Alert. Walking down the street. In full daylight.

And only *she* had heard it. That realization should have shaken her. But it didn't, not in the way she expected. She wasn't afraid of *him* anymore.

What scared Sam now was the *possibility* that none of this was real. That *he* wasn't real. That this was what it felt like to spiral. That this was how madness began.

Sam entered the shop through the back door and made her way to the small table she and Julie used for lunch breaks, and sometimes dinner when they worked late. She sat down and rubbed her temples. Her head throbbed, but worse was the knot forming in her gut.

Should she tell Julie everything?

Probably not. Julie might mean well, but this was the kind of story that ended with someone being gently escorted to a psych ward for "observation." Sam wasn't ready to risk that.

Then she remembered **Dr. West**.

Frantically, she rifled through the small tote she carried everywhere, past pens, napkins, receipts, until her fingers found the edge of a business card.

There.

No way she was calling from the shop. Not with Julie in earshot. *Tonight,* she thought. *Or maybe first thing in the morning before work.* Sam slipped the card back in her tote and headed for her drawing table just as Julie walked up behind her and wrapped her in a hug.

"You find anything at the bookstore?" Julie asked warmly.

Guilt twisted in Sam's chest. *Lying to Julie again. But I've got to keep it cool.*

"Nothing that jumped out at me," she said. "I'll try again sometime. Maybe tomorrow morning. Not sure yet."

Julie leaned against the edge of Sam's table. "Slow morning. Nothing new for a Thursday."

Sam started pulling out designs. "I've got two consults this afternoon, one at four, one at five."

Julie moved around to Sam's front, where she could see her face. "How 'bout we close up early after your last consult and head down to *The Eye Patch*? A couple drinks, girl's'night. No Ronnie."

She tilted her head, one brow raised. Her hand rested on Sam's shoulder.

61

Sam smiled and looked up at the ceiling fan, feigning deep thought. "Hmmm... well, I do have a pretty packed schedule. Gotta advise the President on global diplomacy, then hop over to some alien planet for intergalactic negotiations... I don't know, Jules, I might be booked solid."

Julie rolled her eyes. "So that's a yes?"

"Of course," Sam said with a grin. "Sounds like a rockin' good time."

The rest of the afternoon passed quietly. Sam and Julie worked at their respective tables. Sam's two clients arrived and left on schedule, each excited about their future ink. Julie locked the door and flipped the sign to CLOSED once the last one left.

Sam cleaned her station while Julie swept the lobby.

Then, suddenly:

"Don't keep me waiting, Rebekka. I've waited eighteen years."

The voice exploded in Sam's mind. She gasped, dropping her pencils onto the floor with a loud clatter.

"You okay back there, Sam? You're not breaking stuff, are you?" Julie called from the front.

"Uh... no, I, just dropped some pencils. Clumsy me," Sam replied, her voice shaky.

She scooped the pencils up, placed them on the table with trembling hands, then walked briskly to the bathroom at the back. She stepped inside, shut the door, and locked it.

Leaning over the sink, she whispered, "I'm not making you wait. What are you talking about? You came out of nowhere. I *still* don't know who you are."

The voice returned, smooth and quiet this time, too close, like it was whispering directly into her thoughts:

"You interfere with our meetings when you drink, Rebekka. The pills, *they* interfere too. You know this."

Sam's eyes narrowed. "Whoa, hold up. I can drink when and where I like. And I *don't* take pills. Someone, or something, is lying to you."

But her voice lacked conviction. She sounded like a child arguing with a teacher.

The voice answered with a soft laugh, "Rebekka... you still don't remember me? You *hurt* me when you say things like that. We've been friends for a long, long... *long* time. We've done things together, Rebekka. Things we both enjoyed."

Sam's stomach churned.

"Did things together." The phrase made her skin crawl. It sounded *wrong*. Twisted.

"Don't let your little friend interfere with our meetings, Rebekka."

Sam froze.

That last comment... it sounded like a **threat**.

Until now, the voice had been cryptic, unsettling, *taunting*, yes, but never **directly** threatening. And this... this wasn't a dream.

She clenched the edge of the sink, knuckles going white.

"Why do you think you need a, what do you call it? Ah yes... a *shrink*, Rebekka?"

The voice oozed into her mind, sharp and mocking.

"Do you think you're... losing your mind? Going *mad*?"

It paused.

Then, a darker tone crept in.

"That's almost laughable, Rebekka. Thinking *I'm* some figment of your imagination? That's very funny. Yes. Hilarious."

And then it laughed. Louder and louder, echoing through her head with manic glee.

Sam winced, half expecting Julie to come running, *until she remembered: she's the only one who hears it.* She gritted her teeth, whispering to the mirror, "Shut up. Just shut up…"

Suddenly,

Knock knock knock.

Julie's voice called from the other side of the bathroom door, muffled but chipper.

"You okay in there? You're not giving a pep talk to your number twos, are you?" Julie laughed at her own joke. "Hurry up, I need to tie one on *quick!*"

Sam blinked, took a breath, and mustered a shaky grin.

"You're sick," she said, forcing a weak laugh. "Real sick."

Sam splashed some water on her face, dried it, unlocked the door and stepped out.

"You ready yet? I need a strong one myself," she said, trying to hide the worry twisting her stomach. But part of her, quiet, defiant, said it just to jab at the voice. *Drink this*, she thought. *Like it or not.*

"All set. Let's go!" Julie grinned, handing Sam her tote and pulling open the back door.

They strolled down the street, the summer heat softened by a breeze, the sidewalk humming with leftover sun. The Eye Patch was buzzing when they walked in, but they managed to snag a booth in the back.

Before Sam could even order, Julie flagged the waiter.

"Four shots, for each of us. Open a tab. Tonight's on me."

Sam blinked. "You don't have to pay for mine. I've got it."

"Nope. It's on your girl. I don't get to spoil you often," Julie said, giving her a playful shake and a quick hug.

The evening flew by, laughter spilling freely between them. They drank, joked, teased each other, and cracked up over nothing. The buzz hit them hard, warm and soft like a blanket. Sam felt light. Numb. And, for the first time in weeks, at ease.

"This was a good idea," she said. "I really needed this."

"Oh man, it's midnight. And I think…" Sam squinted at Julie, trying to focus. "…I might be a little drunk."

Julie, swaying in her seat, squinted back. "*Little?* Nah, we ain't drunk yet. We need, like, three more each."

She nearly slid out of her chair, which triggered a whole new round of laughter.

"Okay, okay… maybe we're drunk. Just a little," Julie admitted, wheezing through her grin.

"I've had enough," Sam said, slurring slightly. "I gotta go to work in the morning. My boss is a real hardass if I show up late again."

Julie smirked. "Yeah, I hear she's a *real* B."
They both burst into laughter again.

Eventually, they stumbled their way to the bar to close out. Julie wouldn't even let Sam see the bill.

"It's none of your business," she said, shielding the receipt with her hand like it was a national secret. "I *got* this."

They walked out into the night, the sidewalk mostly empty, the air warm but breezy. Somewhere nearby, a couple chatted about their upcoming vacation. It was peaceful.

Julie turned to Sam. "You want me to call Ronnie to take us home? Or an Uber?"

Sam shook her head. "Nah, I'm a big girl, *Mom*. I live a few blocks away. A walk might do me good. Promise I'll text you when I get home."

Julie gave her a tight hug. "Okay. But if you don't text me, I'm coming to find you. With a stick." They both laughed, parted ways, and drifted toward their respective parts of town, each swaying a little, then walking straighter as the night cooled them down.

Sam headed toward the Fresno uptown area, enjoying the breeze and the quiet. She passed the last intersection before her street. Her building was just about a hundred and twenty-five yards ahead, on the left.

Then she saw the *figure*.

It stepped out, not completely, just hovering at the edge of the shadows, swaying slightly. Shifting left and right. Sam slowed. A surge of fear rose in her chest. Flashbacks hit, *the man from the shop*, the violence, the helplessness. The buzz from the drinks bled away, replaced by cold dread. She thought about crossing the street, but the figure was too close now. Her door was just ahead. She tried to act normal, eyes forward, pace quickening.

"Hey. Hey, you got a dollar? I'm talking to you," the voice called out.

Sam ignored it.

But before she could reach the door, a hand clamped onto her shoulder.

Yanked.

Spun her around.

"Give me your purse," the voice snarled, "before I kill you."

Sam opened her mouth to scream.

Blackness.

The familiar blackness.

The *void*.

The place where *he* lived.

"Hello...? Hey... where are you? Why am I here? Hello... hello..." Sam's voice trailed off into the void.

She was standing in the darkness again, but it wasn't like the other times. This time, she didn't remember falling asleep. She didn't remember dreaming. She didn't remember getting home.

The street. Saying goodbye to Julie. Walking... then what?

Nothing.

After standing there for what felt like hours, she slowly sat down in the black, folding her knees up to her chest.

"I think I'm broken," she whispered into the silence, burying her face in her arms. Sam's eyes fluttered open.

Sunlight. Ceiling. *Home.*

She was in bed. Her bedroom. The pale morning light streaked through the blinds. She sat up slowly, feeling like every muscle had gone soft and sore.

Her feet touched the floor, and then she noticed. Scratches. Thin ones. All along the tops of her feet. *Where the hell...?*

She stumbled toward the bathroom, still half in a daze. When she caught sight of her reflection, she froze. Her eyes were bloodshot, rimmed with darkness. Her cheeks and neck, scratched. Small, shallow nicks like she'd been crawling through underbrush.

She turned on the faucet and splashed her face. The water pooled in the porcelain.

Pink. It was tinged with a soft rose color.

She blinked.

Where's that color coming from?

Sam looked down at her hands, and her stomach turned.

Her fingernails were packed with something black.

Dirt? Mud? No... it looks like...

She scrubbed under her nails, harder and harder. The pink water deepened to a dark rust-red.

Blood. Mud. What is this? Where was I?

A dizzy panic started to well up, but she forced herself to breathe.

"Drunk," she muttered to the mirror. "I must've done something stupid drunk. Passed out in an alley or something. Right?" But she didn't believe it. Not really. She dried her hands, dressed quickly, and sat on the bed. It was still early. Too early for the shop. She pulled Dr. West's business card from her tote and picked up her phone to call, and then it hit her.

Julie.

She never texted Julie last night. She *always* texted. Julie would be worried sick.

Cursing under her breath, she found Julie's contact and pressed "Call." It rang once.

"...Huh? He, hello...? Sam? Is that you?"

"I'm sorry. *So* sorry, Jules. I promised I'd text, but I didn't. I must've just passed out and forgotten. I'll make it up to you, I swear."

Julie chuckled, groggy. "What are you talking about? You *did* text me. About thirty minutes after we left the pub. A bit later than I thought, but no big deal. Girl, you were way more plastered than I realized. Go back to bed. I'm dying. We'll open late. We *own* the place, remember?"

She laughed again and hung up.

Sam just stared at the phone.

I texted her?

She opened her messages.

There it was.

"Hey Jules, I made it home safe and sound. Talk tomorrow. Rebekka."

Sam's heart slowed.

Rebekka. Not Sam.

She hadn't used *that* name in eighteen years. Not since everything happened. Not since *before.* Her hands trembled.

The dreams. The voice. It always calls me Rebekka.

Sam sat on the edge of her bed, staring at the text still glowing on her phone screen.

"Hey Jules, I made it home safe and sound. Talk tomorrow. Rebekka."

I didn't send that.

She knew it deep in her bones. The last thing she remembered was saying goodbye to Julie... then walking...

After that, *nothing.* Just darkness. Not even the voice. No dreamscape. Just... void.

Sam closed the messages app, opened the keypad, and fumbled for Dr. West's business card. She dialed the number.

It rang twice.

"Hello, Dr. West's office, this is Diane. How can I help you today?"

"Um... yeah. I was trying to reach Dr. West. She... she gave me this number. Said I could call anytime. I thought this was a direct line."

"May I ask who's calling? Dr. West is currently with a client, but I can take your name and number for a call back."

"No. No, it's fine. I'll call back later."

"Are you sure? It might be best to, "

"I said I'll call back."

Sam hung up. She didn't like how much her voice had cracked.

Didn't like the thought of leaving her name. Didn't like any of this.

"I *am* losing it," she whispered. "This is what a breakdown feels like."

And then the tears came.

Hot. Silent. Shameful.

She *never* cried. Not anymore. She was hard. Tough. Solid. Crying meant losing.
But now? She didn't even know if she was in control of herself anymore.
If she was still... Sam.

She sat there and let it out.

But when the tears stopped, something settled inside her. A flicker. A growl. A voice, not the one from the dreams, *her* voice.

I'm not going down easy.

Sam stood up, wiped her face, and looked at herself in the mirror.

"I'm not going down easy," she said again.

She washed up, got dressed, and headed out.

With every step toward the shop, she repeated it like a mantra.

"I'm not going down easy."

75

"I'm going to fight."

"I'm still here."

It was ten a.m. sharp when Sam walked through the back door of the shop and straight to her drawing table.

"Hey Julie! I'm here, and *on time*," she called out.

Julie's voice came from the waiting area, sharp with urgency.

"Sam! Sam, come here, you've gotta see this."

Sam stepped out front. Julie was frozen in front of the mounted TV, remote in hand, eyes wide.

"What is it?" Sam asked, already sensing something was wrong.

Julie didn't look away from the screen. "Look. Just… look."

On the TV was a local news broadcast. A breaking story.

"**...the body was discovered just after midnight in an alleyway near Fulton and Harrison, right near the uptown apartments. Police are calling it one of the most gruesome scenes they've ever witnessed...**"

Sam's eyes flicked to the bottom of the screen. *That's my street.*

Julie turned to her, pale. "Sam… that's your neighborhood. Like, *right* by your place."

The anchor continued:

"The male victim, believed to be homeless, was found mutilated and drained of blood. His body was discovered in the upper limbs of a tree, with claw-like lacerations and no signs of defensive struggle..."

Julie's voice was a whisper now. "They said someone from your building heard a woman scream. That's when they called the cops. But by the time officers arrived, it was silent."

Sam felt the blood leave her face. She staggered slightly and dropped into the nearest chair.

Julie sat beside her. "Sam… that could've been you."

Sam didn't answer right away. She *wanted* to say she hadn't heard anything. She *wanted* to say she remembered getting home. She *wanted* to believe it had nothing to do with her.

But that text said *Rebekka.*

Her fingernails were filled with mud. There were scratches on her neck and feet.

And her dreams had turned into blackouts.

"Sam?" Julie's hand was on her back.

"I'm okay," Sam said, barely above a whisper. "I'm… I'm okay."

But even she didn't believe it. Sam looked over at Julie, eyes wide. Her voice trembled just slightly, a current of fear beneath the words.

"Julie... I, I think I'm going to head back home. That story on the news... It's messing with my head. I'm not going to do anything stupid, I promise. I just... I need to clear my mind after what we saw."

Julie placed a hand on Sam's shoulder, her voice soft. "Sam, I get it. I really do. It did''t even happen near my place, and I'm freaked out. But it happened *right by yours*. You're my best friend, of course I'm worried."

Julie turned to the three clients browsing the wall of designs near the waiting area. "Hey guys, and gal, I'm so sorry, but we've had a personal emergency. It's related to what just aired on the news, and we need to close the shop for the day."

One of the customers, a tall woman in a leather jacket, stepped forward. "No worries. I saw the story. Hope your friend's okay."

"Thanks," Julie said, exhaling. "If you come back in the next five days, I'll personally give you twenty-five percent off anything in the yellow book. I really appreciate your understanding."

As they left, Sam quietly gathered her things and slipped out the back door. She didn't want to cry, didn't want to fall apart in front of anyone else. But her thoughts were tangled. The flash of memory, *someone grabbing her shoulder... the man asking for money...* It was so thin. Fragile. Like fog dissipating before you can hold it.

Instead of heading straight home, Sam veered right, toward the electronics store two blocks down. Inside, she found a wall of QLED TVs, most of them running demos or looping sports highlights. She found a remote and flipped through channels until she landed on the local news.

They were still talking about it.

Still talking about him.

"...**authorities have now identified the man as a local transient known to frequent the uptown corridor. The cause of death remains undetermined, though authorities are calling it unusually violent.**"

Sam's heart thumped faster.

"Show his face," she whispered. "Come on. Show him."

As if on cue, the anchor said, "**Police have just released an old mugshot of the victim.**"

The screen cut to a photo: disheveled, early forties, scruffy beard, wide, anxious eyes. A face weathered by time and hardship.

Sam closed her eyes. Concentrated.

"*Hey, you got a dollar?*"

The voice was the same.

But beyond that... nothing. Just black.

Frustrated, she left the store and started her walk home, taking the same route she always did. The streets looked unchanged, cars idling at lights, a woman walking a dog, a guy smoking outside a laundromat, but it all felt wrong. *Like a movie set still standing after the film's over.*

She turned the last corner toward her building, and as her apartment came into view, a sharp flash of memory lit up her mind like lightning.

A figure in the shadows.

"Hey, you, got a dollar?"

Then, *a hand on her shoulder.*

Sam froze in place. The noise of the street dropped away.

"Hey, move, would you? You're standing in our shot." A voice broke through, and a hand tapped her shoulder. Sam spun around.

It was a cameraman, hauling a tripod from the back of a van with a local news logo on the side.

"Sorry," Sam muttered, stepping back instinctively.

The cameraman tilted his head. "You live in this building? You know anything about what happened last night?"

Sam stared at him, eyes unfocused. Then she looked down at her shoes, scuffed and a little dirty. She opened her mouth to speak, then thought better of it. She just walked past him in silence, toward the apartment entrance. Sam opened her apartment door, slipped inside, and locked it behind her. The silence felt heavy, like the air had weight.

Her mind churned. *What happened last night?* The pieces were scattered, like a puzzle dumped onto the floor with no edges to start from. She couldn't call Dr. West yet, not until she knew for sure that she wasn't somehow *involved* with what happened to the man they found.

The voice knows something, she thought.

She moved into the bedroom, her eyes falling on the pill bottle on the nightstand. She didn't want to take one, didn't want the fuzziness, but she also knew the truth, sleep wouldn't come on its own. She picked up the bottle, twisted off the cap, and shook one pill into her hand. *"That should be plenty."* She swallowed it dry, lay down, and stared at the ceiling. Gradually, the world around her darkened, shadows deepening at the corners of her vision, until the blackness wrapped around her like a blanket. She knew what came next.

She was back.

Dark room. Still. Silent.

Alone, for now.

Then the voice.

"Why did you come, Rebekka?" it purred, smooth and smoky, drifting like smoke around her ears.

"I need answers," she said. "Did you send a text from my phone last night?"

"Like I told you, Rebekka... drinking does not benefit us."

"So you sent the message because I passed out drunk and forgot to?" she snapped.

"You think I did it out of concern for your friend? That's very humorous, Rebekka." The voice chuckled, low, dry, echoing through the dark like a whisper bouncing off cavern walls.

"Then why *was* the message sent?"

"I didn't send it. You did. It's you, Rebekka. You're returning. Soon, we'll be the way we used to be."

Sam's voice was cold. "I don't remember sending any message. I *never* use the name Rebekka. That's not me anymore."

The voice responded, softer this time, almost fond.

83

"You were Rebekka. And you will be again."

Sam clenched her fists. *What does that even mean?*

As if reading her thoughts: "In time, it will come back to you. It's already happening. Even now."

She shook her head. "You're not making sense."

The voice paused, then shifted, oily and amused.

"So... how was your night? Did you enjoy it?"

Sam hesitated. "Yeah. I had fun with Julie. Drinking, laughing."

"Oh Rebekka…" the voice crooned, **"…**I'm not talking about your little friend.**"**

A deep, growling laughter followed, low and hungry.

Her stomach twisted.

"Then I guess I don't know what you're talking about," she said, sarcasm sharpening her tone like a blade.

But even as she said it, a cold sweat trickled down her spine.

"Oh, but you do.**"** The voice was closer now, almost brushing against her ear. "You know exactly who I'm referring to, Rebekka.**"**

A pause. Heavy. Expectant. "Did you enjoy it?"

"Enjoy what?! You're not making any sense!"

"I'm not going to spell it out for you, Rebekka. You'll have to come to it on your own. It will help you return."

"I'm done with your games. You're just a figment of my mind, a side effect from years of medication. You don't exist."

"Oh, Rebekka," the voice cooed, "you sound just like Dr. Rinshaw. You remember him, don't you? Always saying you were playing make-believe, that you were doing it for attention. You remember that, Rebekka. Sure you do."

"What? I don't know what you're talking about. I don't know any Dr. Rinshaw!"

The voice ignored her defiance, slipping back into its slow, smooth cadence.

"I have a question you keep avoiding. Who, or what, do you think I am?"

Sam's voice cracked with resolve. "I don't know you."

"Rebekka, you do. We go way back. We've always been close. I'm helping bring you back to me."

"Still avoiding the question," she snapped. "You're nothing but shadows and riddles."

The voice grew quieter, but sharper.

"So... how's your family, Rebekka? Your father... your sweet, sweet mother... and your tasty brother, Jason?"

"*Don't* bring them into this." Her voice had steel in it now, trembling but hard.

"You never answer my questions, Rebekka."

"Were you involved in the death of that homeless man last night?" Sam asked, her voice hollow.

The voice chuckled low and mean.

"That's not like you, blaming others for your own actions."

Sam's fists clenched, her throat burned. "Let me out of here! Let me go!"

She wasn't talking *to* the voice anymore, just shouting into the dark. Talking in circles with this thing was getting her nowhere. The conversation was always a loop. Always a trap.

"You came to me, Rebekka," the voice said calmly. "You can leave anytime you want. I'm not holding you back, not here."

BAM!

Sam jolted upright, eyes wide, heart pounding.

BAM.

The sound came again, the garbage truck outside, lifting and dumping the metal bin onto the pavement.

She sat in her bed, disoriented. Her clock read 1:12 p.m. It had only been about an hour. The pill was still in her system, but she was fully awake now, no chance of drifting back. Her head throbbed, her heart raced. She rubbed her eyes, then pushed herself up.

I'm done.

No more dreams. No more riddles. No more circular conversations with something that may not even exist.

Sam took out her phone and stared at the message she had supposedly sent to Julie. *I seriously don't remember sending that.*

Her thoughts swirled. *I'm still not even sure what happened that night on my way home. I know I saw the homeless man, I remember his question and standing face-to-face with him... but that's all.*

Just as Sam was about to put the phone down, it buzzed in her hand. The sudden vibration startled her so much she nearly dropped it.

Chapter 5 - Dr Rachel West, Psychiatrist

Incoming Call – Dr. West's Office. She tapped the call button. "Hello... this is Sam. Sam Logan."

"Hello, Reb—, sorry, Sam," said a familiar voice. "This is Dr. Rachel West. My receptionist said someone called asking for me and gave me this number. I'm glad it was you. I've been wondering how you were doing."

"Hello, Dr. West..." Sam hesitated. Part of her still debated how much to reveal. She silently kicked herself for not blocking her number when she made the earlier call.

"Uh... yeah, I'm doing... so-so. I haven't had any thoughts of hurting myself or anything like that, but I've been having these dreams. Really strange dreams. And they're making me question... well, " she sighed, "they're making me question my sanity. I mean, I don't know. I don't know if they're from the overdose or long-term effects of sleeping pills or depression meds... I just don't know."

"It does sound like you're experiencing something," Dr. West said gently. "I can't give you any sort of diagnosis without knowing more, what the dreams are, how they feel, when they happen, what's in them. That sort of thing."

She paused, then added, "That said, I've had many patients over the years who reported strange or vivid dreams, especially on certain medications. But your experience sounds... deeper. More personal. If you're willing, I'd like to offer a session where we can do some light memory regression and talk more in detail about what's happening. Nothing invasive. Just guided recall and analysis."

Sam sat on the bed, eyes drifting to the faint scratches on her feet. *Did I already say too much?* She hesitated again, silence stretching on the line.

Dr. West spoke up, her tone calm and kind. "Sam, please don't feel pressured. Like I told you in the hospital, I only want to help if you want help. No pushing, no obligation. Just a door you can walk through, when *you're* ready."

She hesitated, then added, her voice quieter now:

"You remind me of my daughter. She took her life many years ago. I've come to terms with it, but the one thing I can't shake... is that she never reached out. She struggled in silence. I see that same weight in you, Sam. And I want to help *you* the way I couldn't help her."

The words hit Sam like a warm but heavy wave. She didn't know what to say at first. Grief and compassion stirred something in her, something like trust. Something like... hope.

"I'm so sorry, Dr. West. I mean that. About your daughter." She swallowed hard. "And yeah. I think I'd like to come in. I think maybe a session could help me get some kind of insight... into what's going on in my head."

"I'm really glad to hear that, Sam," Dr. West said warmly. "And just to be clear, this session won't cost you anything. You're not a client to me right now, you're a person who needs support. We'll work out the rest later. For now, just focus on being okay."

Dr. West offered to do the session wherever Sam felt most comfortable, her office, or Sam's home. But Sam quickly decided: it needed to be in the office. She couldn't risk anyone spotting Dr.

West at her apartment and asking questions. She already felt like she was barely keeping the threads of her sanity together.

They picked a day and time. After the call ended, Sam sat on the edge of her bed. For the first time in what felt like days, she exhaled. Not everything felt okay, but something felt a little less wrong.

Maybe, she thought, *just maybe, I'll find an answer.*

The next few days were… more normal. No dreams. No voices. Nothing dark or strange clawing at the edge of Sam's mind.
She clung to that normalcy like a lifeline.

She and Julie leaned on each other, trying to move past the murder that happened near Sam's building. It still gave them both chills. They made a quiet pact: no more pub hopping, no more getting plastered for a while. They were both too aware now of what could happen if you weren't in your right mind.

Then the day finally arrived, her visit with Dr. West. Sam woke early that morning and, without really thinking about it, dressed more conservatively than usual. Long-sleeved tee, full-length jeans, and sneakers. She looked at herself in the bathroom mirror and frowned.

"I don't even know why I dressed like this," she muttered. "She's seen me in a hospital gown. She's seen the tats on my arms and legs." She sighed. "I don't want to give anyone the wrong idea about me... I guess."

She arrived at Dr. West's office a little early. The receptionist smiled, scribbled Sam's name on a notepad, *not* the appointment log, and waved toward the seating area. "Feel free to sit anywhere. Would you like some coffee or water?"

"No, I'm good. Thank you." Sam hesitated. "I know I'm early, but... would you mind pointing me to the restroom? I'm kinda nervous, I guess."

The receptionist grinned. "Totally understandable. It's down the hall, first door on the left."

"Thanks," Sam replied, then made her way to the bathroom.

It was a small, single-person restroom. Clean. Plain. No frills.

Just white walls, a mirror, a sink, and a toilet.

She stood in front of the mirror, checking her reflection.

Trying to look... sane. Trying to look like someone normal.

She hadn't told Julie the truth again, another lie. Said she was going to look at new tattoo design books and maybe meet a reporter from an ink mag for lunch.

Lie, lie, lie.

"I hate lying to her," Sam whispered. "But I'm not telling her I'm seeing a head shrink."

She double-checked her hair, wiped under her eyes. She hadn't worn much makeup, on purpose. If she cried, she didn't want streaks of eyeliner running down her face. And honestly? She didn't like makeup anyway.

She turned toward the door, hand on the knob. Then came the voice.

"Do you think she'll stamp you sane, Rebekka?"

The sound was sharp, condescending.

94

"Is this going to help you ignore me, Rebekka? You still think I'm a figment of your imagination?"

Sam froze.

Not dreaming. Not asleep.

Not even lying down.

This was real. She was awake. She clenched her jaw and whispered, just once:

"I'm not responding to you. You'll be gone soon. Bye."

The voice laughed. A low, cold, smoky laugh that echoed inside her skull. "I think not, Rebekka. We, *you and I*, just got back together."

Sam shook her head, opened the bathroom door, and stepped out into the hallway.

Back in the waiting room, the receptionist was still on the phone but covered the receiver with her hand and gave Sam a polite nod.

"She'll be with you in just a minute."

Sam gave a wordless smile, sat down, and stared straight ahead.

The voice was still there, coiled like smoke in the back of her mind.

But she wasn't going to feed it.

The door to the back office opened, and Dr. West stepped out with a warm smile.

"Good morning, Sam. I'm so glad you came in today."

She turned to the receptionist. "Hold any calls while I'm with Sam. If it runs into lunch, feel free to take your break."

Sam stepped into the office, and Dr. West followed, closing the door gently behind her.

"You look different today," the doctor said as she crossed the room. "Didn't think you were the type to cover up all your ink. You have some beautiful tattoos, some very *interesting* ones."

Sam glanced down at her long sleeves. "Yeah... I usually don't dress like this. I guess I just wanted to look, I don't know... normal? Especially to the people downstairs, or your receptionist."

She felt silly admitting it. A little ashamed. It wasn't like her to care what others thought. That had always been Julie's worry, not hers.

"Sam," Dr. West said kindly, "you should always be *you.* You're a beautiful woman. Your tattoos are a part of you. Don't cover them up for someone else's idea of who you should be."

She gave Sam a gentle hug, then walked to her desk, retrieved a notebook, and moved over to a pair of plush chairs near the window. She motioned to one of them. "Sit here, across from me. I want us to be eye-to-eye today. No one's above or below anyone here, we're equals."

Sam nodded and sat in the chair. It looked stiff, but to her surprise, it was just right, high-backed, soft, supportive. Her feet pressed firmly into the rug beneath.

Dr. West smiled and settled into the other chair. "So... tell me, Sam. How are you feeling today, mentally and physically?"

Sam hesitated, glancing around the room. Her eyes caught on a photo beside the doctor's desk, a younger girl, maybe sixteen or seventeen, hugging Dr. West. *Her daughter*, Sam guessed.

Sam felt guilty but said, "Well, um, I'm okay today."

"That's not like you, Rebekka," the voice whispered, almost gently, almost mocking. "Lying has become second nature now, hasn't it?"

Sam's eyes flicked to the window. There, just outside, was a fountain. An angel stood in the center, wings stretched wide. The sound of the water bubbling was soft, almost like a whisper.

She blinked hard, trying to hold herself together. Trying to stay present.

"Well, that's not a very good start, Sam." Dr. West leaned forward slightly. "Your body language doesn't match your words. You're tense, hands gripping your knees, and you keep looking anywhere but at me."

Sam felt a sting of guilt, but also a strange sense of comfort. Dr. West saw right through her.

"Let's try that again, shall we?" Dr. West said. The doctor looked her in the eyes. "So, Sam… how are you feeling today, *really*?"

Sam's instinct was to look away again, out the window, but she stopped herself.
Instead, she moved her hands to the thick arms of the chair, gripping them tightly.

Don't break down. Don't break down. Don't break down.

"I... I'm not good, Dr. West. I feel like I'm losing my grip on reality."

A single tear escaped her left eye, and she wiped it away quickly.

"Go on, Sam," Dr. West said gently, scribbling something in her notebook.

"I, uh... ever since the hospital incident... "

"You're referring to your suicide attempt?" Dr. West's tone remained soft. "You can say it. There's no shame here."

She reached over and placed a calming hand on Sam's.

"Yeah... since I tried to take my life."

Another tear threatened, but Sam caught it before it fell.

"Ever since then, I've been having these... strange dreams. Not every night, but most. Sometimes it's just darkness, pure black. I know I'm in something like a room, but there are no walls. At least none I can see. And then... the voice shows up."

"Tell me about the voice," Dr. West prompted.

"It's deep. Smooth. Hypnotic, almost. I know it's not me talking, and not anyone I know, or think I know. It should scare me, I think. But it doesn't. And that... that freaks me out a little."

Her hands were still gripping the chair arms so tightly that her knuckles were pale.

"What makes you feel like you *should* be afraid of it?" Dr. West asked, making another note. "Has it ever threatened you?"

"No. Not directly. But it *feels* like it wants something. I don't know what. It avoids questions, especially when I ask what or who it is."

Dr. West leaned back slightly, watching Sam carefully.

"So, what makes you think the voice is a bad thing? Could it be some kind of internal guide? A comforting part of yourself, trying to help you process your life or your trauma?"

"No." Sam shook her head. "It's not trying to help. It's... familiar somehow, but not in a good way. It *always* asks about my family, my dad, my mom... my brother."

Her voice trembled as she spoke.

Dr. West noted the change instantly. "Why does it bother you when it brings up your family, Sam? Did something happen between you and them? When was the last time you spoke to your parents or your brother?"

Sam's knee started bouncing, unaware. Her eyes began to well up again.

"I'm sorry, Sam," Dr. West said gently. "Did I hit something sensitive? A memory?"

"No, it's okay. You don't have all the history. You couldn't know."
She paused, tears now flowing freely.
"My family... they died when I was nine. I don't remember the accident. Nothing about it. Not even the month before, or after. It's just... gone. A black hole in my memory."

Dr. West reached for a nearby side table and handed her a small box of tissues.

"Thank you," Sam whispered, taking one and dabbing her face. But the tears wouldn't stop.

"I can't even remember what they looked like," she said, voice cracking.

"No one ever told me what happened. And after the accident... all my blood relatives just... cut me off. Even my grandparents. They didn't want me."

Her words came in fits now, sobs mixing with sentences.

"Sam," Dr. West said, "we can pause."

"No. No, I want to finish. I want it *out*. It's been in me too damn long."

She wiped her eyes harder this time, smearing what little makeup she'd put on.

"My grandparents disowned me. After the accident, I never saw them again. Never saw *any* family again. I was in foster care until I aged out at eighteen. Nine years I bounced around. I got to the point I didn't even want to *know* the families I was with. I just kept to myself. Closed off. Shut down."

Her voice quieted.

"I didn't have any real friends until I met Julie. Sure, I had people I *knew*, acquaintances, coworkers, but Julie was the first person who actually gave a damn."

She took a deep breath, wiped her face again.

"It doesn't matter what my makeup looks like. I'm not putting any more of it on today."

Dr. West gave her a soft smile. "So you've been a loner since you were nine. Independent. Guarded. That makes a lot of sense now. Julie must be pretty important to you."

"She is," Sam said, then raised an eyebrow at the doctor's next question.

"Is she your girlfriend?"

Sam let out a half-chuckle, eyes widening. "What? No. No way. She *wishes.*"

She shook her head, wiping away the last of her tears.

"I'm not lesbian, or bi, or any of that nonsense. I'm straight. I just don't... want relationships right now. I've got too much going on. I'm focused on me and tattooing. That's it."

Dr. West nodded. "Understood. I only asked because, at the hospital, she seemed fiercely protective of you."

"Yeah, she's got that 'mother hen' vibe. She thinks it's her job to save me or something."

They both laughed softly.

Dr. West flipped to a clean page in her notebook. "So... we've covered your history, your childhood, your trauma, your friendship with Julie. Some medical background, too. But we haven't touched on two very important things."

Sam looked up, eyes curious but wary.

"We don't know why you *weren't* dreaming at all before your hospitalization. And we don't know what happened to your memories from age nine."

She leaned forward, voice soft but firm. "Sam... would you be willing to explore those missing memories with me? We can use a very light form of regression. Nothing invasive. You'll be completely conscious, in control, and safe. But it might help us uncover what's buried."

Sam blinked, then slowly nodded.

"I'm tired of not knowing," she said. "If it helps me figure out what's real... then yeah. Let's do it."

Dr. West led Sam over to the couch, long, fluffy, but firm. Sam lay down, head resting on a pillow, the Kleenex packet resting lightly on her chest. Dr. West described the session they were about to undertake, her voice calm and even. She asked Sam if she was comfortable, too cold or hot, or if she wanted water before they began.

Sam nodded. "No, I'm fine. Ready to proceed."

"Okay, Sam," Dr. West began, pausing between each area of the body, letting Sam settle each time. "Close your eyes and relax. Relax your toes, ankles, and legs. Let them feel loose. Let the tension dissipate. Now your hips, lower torso... relaxed. Your upper body and arms, loose and tension-free. Your neck and head... relaxed. You're now floating above your body, relaxed and free. Can you still hear me, Sam?"

"Mmmhuh, yeah... I can hear you, Dr. West."

"Good. You're floating above your body now, and we want to enter your mind. You can see a projector in your mind. Do you see it, Sam?"

"Umm-hmm... yes."

"Good, Sam, very good. Click on the projector now. Let it go in reverse, past the last few weeks... the weeks turn into months. Do you see them reversing, Sam? Do you see yourself getting younger?"

"Umm... yessss..."

Sam's responses were slow, like she was teetering on the edge of sleep.

"Good, Sam. The reel is slowing now. It's getting close to when you were eight years old."

Sam was quiet, her arms limp at her sides, breathing deep and steady. A single tear slid from her eye.

"What's wrong, Sam? Why are you crying?"

Dr. West bent forward, gently dabbing the tear from Sam's temple.

"I'm alone. My Grams and Paw don't want me. No one wants me."

"It's okay, Sam. We're going before that. Let the reel continue back further, to when you were eight. Has it stopped now, Sam?"

"Y-yes."

"Sam, do you see your eight-year-old self? What do you see?"

"I... I see Jason. He's three. He's running through the sprinklers in the front yard, and I'm chasing him."

"Who else is there, Sam? Do you see anyone else?"

"Yes... Mommy and Daddy. They're sitting on the swing together, watching me and Jason."

"Is there anyone else? An uncle, grandparent, or friend?"

"No. Just us. The fireflies are out. Let's catch them, Jason. I'll help you."

"Sam, can you still hear me?"

"Y...yes."

"Good. Let's move the reel forward now, slowly. Let's go to your ninth birthday. Can you see it yet? Stop the reel at your ninth birthday."

"Okay. I'm nine today. Mommy said I'm going to have a party."

Her voice had shifted, high-pitched and childlike.

"That's good, Sam. Happy birthday. Who is at your party? Who do you see?"

"Mommy, Daddy, Jason, Freda, Bobby, Aunt Ronda, Uncle John."

"Very good, Sam. Tell me, who are Freda and Bobby? Are they cousins or friends?"

"Freda and Bobby are my cousins. They come over sometimes. Aunt Ronda and Uncle John are their parents. I think Aunt Ronda is Mommy's sister."

"That's good, Sam. Are your grandparents there? Do you see Grams and Paw?"

"No, they're not here. But they sent me a present."

"That's nice. Are there any other children or adults there? Any school friends?"

Tears started to fall from Sam's eyes.

"I don't have any friends. Mommy and Daddy won't let me. I'm bad."

Dr. West gently wiped the tears, leaned in, and scribbled in her notebook.

"Why would they say you're bad, Sam? Did you do something wrong?"

Sam didn't answer.

"Sam, can you still hear me? Can you hear my voice?"

"Yes..."

"That's good. Why are you bad, Sam? Why did your parents say that?"

"Because I have a friend."

Dr. West quickly wrote more notes.

"Sam, who is your friend?"

"I'm a bad girl because I have a friend."

Sam's breathing began to speed up, shallow and fast. Her body tensed.

"Sam, if you can hear me, who is your friend?"

"The shadow man in the corner. He said he's my friend. Mommy and Daddy don't like me to have friends."

"Sam, this shadow man, do you know him? Is he someone you've seen before?"

"He's my friend. I drew him. I like to draw. He made me draw him."

Dr. West leaned in and whispered, "Sam, relax. You're watching a reel. You aren't there. You're just observing from a distance. You are safe."

Sam's breathing slowed.

"Sam, can you hear me?"

"Yes, Dr. West. I can hear you."

"That's good. Sam, can you describe the shadow man?"

"Red eyes. He has red eyes. He's dark and formless, like black or gray smoke."

Dr. West scribbled furiously.

"Let's move the reel forward, slowly, ever so slowly. What do you see, Sam?"

"The shadow man... he told me to do something bad."

Dr. West's concern grew. Sam's breathing slowed dangerously, five shallow breaths a minute. Too slow.

"Sam, this is Dr. West. Sam, move your hand if you can hear me."

"The shadow man said to do it. I will do it. He's my friend forever."

"Sam. Sam, if you can hear me, lift a finger. This is Dr. West. You must answer me."

A slight twitch from Sam's hand.

"Good. Sam, I'm going to count to three. When I reach three, you will wake. One... two... listen to me, Sam... three."

Sam's eyes flickered open, blinking slowly.

"How did I do, Dr. West? Sorry, I'm not great with hypnosis. Maybe next time."

She sat up and smiled sheepishly.

Dr. West closed her notebook slowly.

"Um... you did very well, Sam. You were an excellent patient. Everything went fine. I think we made a small bit of progress."

"That's a relief." Sam sighed. "I don't remember anything. Not a drop. I thought I didn't even go under. I remember lying on the couch, you talking, and then you told me to wake up."

"That's okay, Sam. You did just fine."

"So... did we find anything interesting? I mean, I didn't say anything too crazy, right?"

"You mentioned something about a shadow man. Do you remember having an imaginary friend when you were young? Before your family passed?"

Sam looked at the doctor, then up at the ceiling, then back.

"No... nothing. Why?"

Dr. West studied Sam's face for a moment, weighing her next words carefully. "During the regression, you described a 'shadow man' with red eyes like smoke, or something close to it. You said he was your friend... that he told you to draw him.

That he made you feel loved, even when your family didn't approve."

Sam's smile faded. "That's… disturbing. I don't remember anything like that, not at all." She fidgeted, wiping her palms on her jeans. "Are you sure I wasn't just dreaming or… making it up?"

"I can't say for sure," Dr. West said gently, "but it felt consistent with deep-seated memory, not fantasy. Children sometimes manifest their trauma through imagined friends or figures. But the clarity in your description, the emotion… it didn't seem imagined."

Sam looked down at her lap, the confusion on her face slowly morphing into unease. "He… he said I was bad because I had a friend. That's what I said?"

Dr. West nodded. "Yes. You also mentioned that your parents didn't want you to have friends. That's troubling. Especially if they isolated you."

"My parents weren't like that," Sam said, shaking her head, but her voice lacked conviction. "I mean… I don't think they were."

"You also mentioned doing something for the shadow man. Something he told you to do."

Sam's stomach turned. "What did I do?"

"You didn't say," Dr. West replied, voice low and serious. "But you called it a 'task, 'and you said when it was complete, he would be with you forever."

Sam's breathing picked up slightly, her thoughts racing. "So now I have some childhood demon boyfriend telling me what to do? That's messed up."

Dr. West smiled softly, trying to cut the tension. "That's one interpretation. But more likely, we're dealing with a manifestation of trauma, a figure that became a coping mechanism, and now may be resurfacing because of unresolved memories."

Sam looked away, toward the window again. The angel fountain shimmered under the sunlight. "Or maybe," she whispered, "he was real."

Dr. West's expression didn't change, but she jotted something in her notebook. "Sam... would you be open to exploring deeper regression in our next session? Only if you're comfortable. You were already near a breakthrough today."

Sam didn't answer right away. Her mind was swimming. Something about this all felt like a door she wasn't sure she wanted to open.

Finally, she said, "Yeah. I want to know what I've been hiding from... and who, or what, this thing is. If it's just in my head, I want to crush it. But if it's not..."

"If it's not?" Dr. West prompted.

"Then I need to know what it wants. Before it takes more than it already has."

Sam and Dr. West discussed when to schedule the next session, one where they could go deeper into the memories.

"What do I do in the meantime, Doctor? I mean, what do I do when I have these dreams? I'm concerned it might convince me to do something. I'm more worried now. More than before." Concern was written all over Sam's face.

"You're an adult now, Sam, and as an adult, you know how to fight back, how to hold your ground. You might try confusing the voice, stifling it in the dream. Just for a few days. I think you'll do fine, but if not, call me and we'll work through it together."

Dr. West scribbled something on a sticky note from her desk. "If for any reason you need to reach me directly, not the office, call this number." She handed the note to Sam. "This is my *real* direct line. Day or night, I'll answer."

Sam took the sticky note and slid it into her tote. "I'll add it to my contacts when I get home. Thank you, Dr. West. Coming here was hard, but... It's been insightful. Helpful." Sam gave a small smile. "I'll see you at the next session."

"You're very welcome, Sam. I'll see you in a few days. And remember, day or night, call if you need me."

"I will." Sam opened the door and walked into the waiting area. The receptionist smiled at her.

"Are we seeing you again soon?" the receptionist asked, taking out her appointment book.

"Yeah, I think the doctor has it scheduled," Sam slowly responded, walking towards the door.

"Great. Have a good rest of your day!" the receptionist responded as she watched Sam exit through the lobby door and into the hallway.

"Thanks. You, too." Sam returned the smile, then turned away, thinking, *I wonder how many patients she says that to. It's a head shrink's office, probably a revolving door of messed-up loons.* Sam smirked at the thought.

She headed home to change before going to the shop. She could only imagine the ribbing she'd get if she showed up in these duds.

Back at her apartment, Sam changed clothes, freshened up in the bathroom, and gave herself a quick once-over in the mirror.

"You even look better after that," she said to her reflection, giving it a wink before heading out.

At the shop, Sam came in through the back door and made her way to her drawing table. She grabbed a pile of designs and started reviewing and editing them.

"Well, look what the cat dragged in," Julie said, walking up behind her and ruffling Sam's short black hair. "Did you find anything you liked? Any fresh ideas? Oh! Are you gonna be featured in another *Ink* magazine?"

Sam spun around in her chair. "Yes, yes, and no," she replied with a smirk.

"Aww, I was hoping it was a new feature. You know that'd be good for business." Julie pouted, sticking out her bottom lip dramatically. "Maybe you can show me some of those fresh new ideas once you sketch them out?"

"Sure thing." The lie tasted bitter in Sam's mouth. She couldn't even look at Julie when she lied, it felt worse every time.

"So, you and Ronnie going out tonight? I heard this is your four-month anniversary. Dang, you two are practically married already."

Sam laughed. Julie raised an eyebrow and stuck out her tongue. "And *yes*, we're going out. Wanna tag along? I'm sure Ronnie won't mind, he thinks you're kinda cool. Not as cool as me, of course. But who is?"

That cracked Sam up. "Oh yeah, I *love* being the third wheel. That's my dream."

The last bit came out darker than intended, bitter

even, bringing thoughts of the black room and her "shadow friend."

The afternoon slipped into evening, and a few walk-ins browsing the stacks of designs and photos. Julie stopped by Sam's station.

"You sure you're going to be okay tonight, closing and all? We can make it later."

"No, Jules, I'll be fine. As soon as the clock hits eleven, I'll lock the door and flip the sign. You go out and have fun, it's your anniversary." She gave Julie a wide grin.

"If you need me for *a-n-y-t-h-i-n-g*, call me. We'll be close by, no more than a block or two."

"I promise, I'll call if anything happens, or if I just get bored."

"You better. Don't make me get the ruler out."

Sam wrinkled her nose. "Promise? You're so kinky."

They both laughed. Julie gave Sam a quick hug and walked out the back door, headed home to change before spending the evening with Ronnie.

And Sam… Sam was left alone in the empty shop, just her and her thoughts.

"This evening better go by quick and quiet. I don't want to use Woody on anyone, but I will." She reached under her station chair, beneath the cloth, and pulled out her Louisville Slugger torpedo bat, tapping it a few times for good luck.

"If someone comes lookin' for trouble, trouble's what they're gonna find."

The rest of the evening stayed quiet. Two teenage girls came in, poking around and asking questions, but left unhappy after Sam told them she couldn't tattoo minors without a parent or guardian present.

Lost a little money there, but she wasn't about to have someone's mom showing up at the shop screaming because her kid got inked without permission.

Promptly at eleven PM, Sam locked the doors, flipped the sign, and shut off all the lights and window signage. She moved slowly tonight, letting her mind coast through the day's activities, thinking about the session at Dr. West's office and all they had discussed.

Sam swept the floors, dusted the counter, cleaned the glass cases, and tidied the bathroom. She and Julie usually flipped a coin to see who'd get stuck with that job. Most of the time, only they used it, but occasionally, a client getting a tattoo would ask to use it if they started feeling nauseated. Tonight, the coin toss was between her... and her.

It was ten minutes till midnight when she exited the back door, locked up, and started walking home. She strolled down the sidewalk, watching the streetlights flicker and fade, letting her thoughts wander.

She thought about her childhood. Did she remember having friends back then, before? There were schoolmates, sure, but no sleepovers, no pool parties, no birthday invitations. Just other kids in class. The thought went deeper. Did she remember *anyone* other than family at her birthday parties? Over during the summers? Before?

I don't remember any friends... not even a red-eyed friend.

She made it back to her apartment without incident. After locking the door behind her, she kicked off her shoes and checked the fridge for a snack or something to drink. One lonely Red Bull sat on the shelf, probably expired.

"If I want to sleep, Red Bull's a hard no. Guess I need to visit the store. I'm kind of short on food and drink," she mumbled aloud.

Instead of looking further, she headed to the bathroom, washed her face, changed into her night clothes, and crawled into bed. She lay there a while, mind still drifting, eyes tracing the familiar cracks in the ceiling. A small part of her was apprehensive. *He* might be there. Waiting for her in the dark.

Eventually, Sam drifted off to sleep.

This time, instead of the black room, she found herself inside an old house. Birthday streamers hung from the ceiling and door frames. There were presents on the table and a Barbie cake placed at the center. She wasn't sure where she was, it seemed familiar, yet somehow different.

She wandered through the house.

In the kitchen, a woman's apron hung on a hook, and dishes were stacked in the sink. Down the hallway, the first door on the right opened into a little girl's room, bright and inviting, Barbie dolls and plush toys scattered across a small twin bed covered in a Barbie-themed bedspread.

The next door on the left was a toddler's room. A small bed close to the floor, popper toys, blocks, and a Lightning McQueen comforter. A toy chest lined the wall.

The final door on the right was the master bedroom, neutral tones, a large bed, a TV stand, a dresser, and nightstands. But no family photos. Despite the birthday party decorations, the house felt cold. Not like a home, just a shell.

As Sam returned to the den, a chill slipped over her skin. Something felt wrong.

In the far-left corner of the room, a shadow loomed, like smoke caught in a fan's updraft.

"You found me, Rebekka. Welcome home. Does this house stir any memories?"
The voice was smooth, gentle, almost caressing.

"I-I don't recognize this place. It feels familiar but... not. Why am I here? Where's the black room?"

"I needed to urge you along. Your memories are so... disjointed. You need my help pulling them together."

"Where's the family that lives here? What did you do to them?"

"Ah, Rebekka, once again, I did nothing. *You* should ask, 'What did *Rebekka* do to them?'"

Sam cringed.

"I don't even know this place. How could I do something to anyone?"

"Come now, Rebekka. Don't be so coy. You should be proud. You do excellent work, so precise."

She had no idea what the voice was talking about, but at this point, she didn't want to know. A heavy feeling settled in her gut. She needed to get out of that house.

"Let me go! Let me out! You're just a figment. You don't control me, you *can't* affect me."

The voice chuckled.

"Oh, but I *can*, and I *do*, Rebekka. You're free to leave any time."

Sam's eyes opened.

Morning light streamed through the window in her bedroom.

She was tired, like she'd slept too long, or too hard.

But this time, the dream was different.

Not just *different*, she could remember it.

Chapter 6 - Home Sweet Home

Sam got up, showered, got dressed, and headed out, not to the shop, but back to the internet café. She wanted to find out what really happened to her family. Her *real* family. Back in the town where she was born and raised for the first nine years of her life: Chester, Connecticut, near Cedar Lake.

A place Sam hadn't seen since being placed in foster care.

Chester was your typical small town. One grocery store, no big-name department chains or box stores, just mom-and-pop places like *Mary's Toy Store* and *His and Hers Clothes for Kids*. Chester was old, established in 1836. It was the kind of town people dreamed of living in, but most couldn't afford to, because nothing was close by, and unless you worked in the logging industry, it was hard to find a job that paid enough to survive.

Sam's now-forgotten relatives likely still lived there. Her aunts, uncles, grandparents, all somewhere in or around Chester. The men worked the logging mills, the women stayed home, raised the kids, and kept house. That was life in Chester, and it had been Sam's life too, for a while.

She made her way to the internet café, paid for an hour, and sat at the same table in the back, her chair positioned so her back faced the wall. She didn't quite know what she was looking for, not yet, but she knew she had to dig. She had to search her past. To find out who the voice was.

And what did it have to do with her?

Sam searched the city records available online. Not everything was there, but enough, maybe just enough to find bits and pieces from the time she lived in Chester with her real family.

She located the archives of the *Chester Daily Observer*, the local newspaper, and dove into the obituary listings. She wasn't interested in any recent deaths that might, or might not, be connected to her. She wanted to go back. Eighteen years back. To the year it happened.

"2006… that should be close," Sam whispered to herself. *It's got to be here.*

Slowly, she scrolled through the obits, eyes scanning every line, every name. She couldn't remember the names of her relatives. Not even her parents. Just Jason's.

She didn't *want* to see an obituary for Jason. Not really. That part of her had long been sealed away, buried deep so she wouldn't have to feel it. But Dr. West's session had cracked that door open.

And now the grief was leaking back in.

She was nearly to the end of the short list of names for 2006 when doubt started to creep in.

Could it have been another year? Earlier? Later? No... it had to be 2006.

Sam bit her lip as she meticulously scrolled. And then, there, at the bottom of the page, she saw it:

Logan, Harry

Logan, Mary E.

Logan, Jason J.

Sam froze.

She stared at the screen, her fingers hovering over the mouse, struggling to find the courage to click. Finally, she did. The page loaded. There they were. Her family, her *real* family. Her father. Her mother. Her little brother.

The obituary didn't list a cause of death. No mention of a car accident. No house fire. No illness. Just the names, the dates, the services. It was clinical. Vague. Almost like the details were purposely omitted.

But something stood out. Her father, *he was Native American.* Memories fluttered at the edge of her mind. His dark black hair. His deep, sharp eyes. *Those eyes.*

"I'm half Native American," Sam whispered to herself.

She smiled, unexpectedly. For once, a detail that felt like *hers.* Something to claim. Strength. Identity. *Roots.* There was no mention of his tribe, but it said there would be a native ritual after the funeral. That piece alone made Sam sit a little straighter. Like some hidden part of herself had just stirred.

She clicked on her mother's name next, **Mary E. Logan**. The photo wasn't necessary. Sam didn't need it. As soon as the name came up, the floodgates opened. Their faces came rushing back. Her mother's laugh. Her grace. Her warmth. The way she'd let Sam brush her long, blonde hair. It hit like a wave.

Then came the hardest click of all.

Jason J. Logan.

The page loaded, and there he was. That little blonde head. Light freckles across his nose. In the photo, he was holding his favorite toy, the one he used to sleep with.

"Jason..." Sam whispered, voice catching. "Oh, Jason... I miss you, little bro."

A tear slipped from her cheek, landing on the keyboard with a soft *tap*. The screen suddenly blinked.

Your session has expired. Please see attendant to purchase more time.

Sam leaned back in the chair and exhaled, long and heavy.

"That was my family."

Sam got up from the table and walked past the attendant's desk.

"Are you okay, miss?" the young-looking attendant asked. He'd noticed the redness in Sam's eyes.

"I'm fine. No problem. Just a side effect of too much computer time, I guess."

The attendant nodded, accepting her answer, and went back to his handheld gaming console.

Sam exited the café and headed toward the shop. Her mind was still turning over the newly recovered memories, and the sad confirmation from the obituaries. Yet, somehow, the world looked different in the mid-morning sun. The sky was bluer, the clouds puffier, and the air fresher. There was something new inside her now, a sense of self she hadn't known existed.

"I wonder what tribe I am," she said softly, smiling to herself. "This calls for a new tat... something to remind me of my heritage."

Sam walked through the back door of the shop, dropped her tote on her drawing table, and went to find Julie.

"Jules! I just found out something incredible!"

Julie came through the separator curtain, a curious smile on her face. "What's that, Sam?"

"You can't say anything to anyone yet, okay? I have to get more info first."

"Alright, alright, don't keep me hanging." Julie planted a hand on her hip, mock-impatient.

"I'm part Native, Native American! Isn't that amazing? I don't know which tribe yet, but I'll find out. I'm so stoked. Aren't you?" Sam's face glowed with excitement. Her smile was wide, her eyes bright.

Julie blinked, surprised. "Whoa, hold on. What are you talking about? Who told you that? Don't tell me you went to that phone-in palm reader on Second Street?"

Sam rolled her eyes. "Come on, you know me better than that. I... I remembered something. Just a small piece." Sam didn't want to mention searching obituaries or digging into the past she'd once said she wanted nothing to do with. Years ago, she'd told Julie about the foster care, the isolation, the blank space where her early memories should've been, but Julie wouldn't understand why she was reopening that door now.

Julie's playful expression faded into concern. "How did this memory come back? Did you hit your head in the shower or fall out of bed? How do memories just... resurface?"

Sam could see the shift in her friend's expression, concern replacing joy. Her own smile dimmed. "Can't I just have a good memory come back without getting grilled? Can't you be happy for me?"

Julie's smile disappeared completely. "Sam, I *am* happy... I just... I'm worried. I want you to be okay. Where did this memory come from, really? You're not... you're not taking those pills again, are you? You promised you were done with that."

The happiness drained from Sam's face, replaced by a cold flash of anger.

"Did you seriously just ask me that? *Accuse* me of using again? Are you f'ing, kidding me?"

She grabbed her tote.

"I just wanted to share something important with you. Something I *remembered*, after eighteen years of nothing. I thought you'd celebrate with me, not interrogate me." Sam turned, storming toward the back door.

"I'm going out. You can close without me today." The door slammed behind her.

"Wow... I didn't see that coming," Julie said to herself. She felt concern for Sam but also guilty, she'd taken Sam's high point and stomped all over it. She thought about calling and apologizing but decided to let Sam cool off first. Sam had a mean temper, it didn't last long, but when it flared, it was fierce.

Sam, no longer riding high on her rediscovered heritage, was still fuming. She couldn't understand why Julie hadn't just been excited for her. She finally had a connection to her past, a *good* connection, and Julie couldn't set aside her concerns long enough to celebrate with her.

"Yes, she *should* celebrate with us, Rebekka. But she thinks it's bad... that *you're* bad for knowing."

The voice, soft, malevolent, stroked Sam's anger like a pet.

Sam didn't even realize at first that it was *the* voice. It felt like *her* voice.

133

"She turned on you, Rebekka. A real friend would be happy for you."

Sam's fists clenched. But then she paused, *that wasn't* her voice. She would never turn on Julie. And Julie would never turn on her.

It's trying to trick me. Trying to drive a wedge.

"You need to leave me alone," Sam said under her breath. "You're a figment. You'll be gone in a few days."

She physically clenched her jaw and forced her thoughts back into place. By the time she reached her apartment building, the anger had mostly faded. She was still miffed at Julie, sure, but not mad anymore. In hindsight, she could understand why Julie was concerned. Sam *had* been lying about where she was going, what was happening to her. And she *had* struggled with pills in the past. Of course, Julie would worry.

I'll apologize tomorrow, Sam thought. *Again.* She sighed. *No one else I'd trust to ink my new Native American tat, anyway. Except for myself.*

She let herself into the apartment and flopped into her only comfy chair in the corner.

"The voice," she whispered. "The shadow man, he tried to trick me. Tried to turn me against my best friend." A shiver ran across her shoulders. She felt violated, almost like something had tried to *use* her.

I need to be more careful with my thoughts. Especially when I'm emotional.

She got up and checked the fridge. Still nothing but that ancient, possibly glowing, Red Bull. Her stomach growled in protest.

"I hear ya," she muttered. "Yeah, yeah, let's go to the store. So excited… yay." She rolled her eyes and mimed tying a noose around her neck. "Let's go before I change my mind."

She left the apartment and walked two blocks *south*, the opposite direction of the shop. She didn't want to risk running into Julie. Not yet.

Nguyen's Corner Market was still open. She grabbed rice noodles, assorted veggies, chopped chicken, and two types of broth. Time to whip up her famous garlic chili chicken noodle soup, famous, at least, to her and Julie. She even picked up vegan ingredients to make a second batch. And a twelve-pack of green tea to go with it.

At checkout, old Mr. Tjen smiled at her.

"Where you been? Thought one of your dragon tattoos ate you!" he joked.

Sam laughed. *He's such a sweet guy,* she thought. *Too bad I can't understand half of what he says. That's on me. I should learn his language. I bet he's even funnier in it.*

As she left the store, headed home with arms full of groceries, she saw *him.*

The guy.

The one who beat her senseless at the shop that night.

She froze.

That's him. Bald head. Bat wings on the back of his head. I know it's him.

Even with her hands full, she followed him, at a distance, wanting to see where he lived. *Let the cops come pick his sorry, woman-beating ass up.*

"I didn't think he lived this close to me," she whispered, a mix of anger and unease swirling in her gut.

They crossed in front of Nguyen's and walked down to the next intersection. He turned onto Suez Street, went all the way to the end, then crossed over into the rundown *Grande Motel*.

Sam stopped at the corner and memorized the name and cross street.

Not going in there, she thought. *Not carrying all this. But I'll write it down the second I get home.*

She turned around, retraced her steps to Nguyen's, and then back to her apartment.

Once inside, she dropped the groceries in the kitchen, popped open a green tea, and scribbled down the motel name and address.

The cops already have his description, she thought. *But I'll make sure to jog their memory when I call.*

Sam stirred around in the kitchen, finishing up her dinner, and the vegan option she planned to bring to Julie tomorrow. The *I'm sorry* dinner. She hummed a tune she'd heard playing at the shop a few days ago. She didn't know the name, but it was catchy.

"Just needs a little more heat," she muttered, "just a small chop of ghost pepper should seal the deal."

She sliced up a quarter of the pepper and stirred it into her pot. Then, with a sly grin, she added the rest into Julie's veggie version.

"A little kick in the butt for *being* a butt."

Sam laughed at the thought.

While the pot simmered on the stove, she dug through her junk drawer and found the detective's business card: **Det. Buk Rogers**, like Buck Rogers, but spelled differently. He'd made that joke when they met, and she'd had no clue what he was talking about. Later, she looked it up: some old sci-fi show from the '80s about a guy who traveled through time to the far future.

She punched in the number.

"Hello, this is Detective Rogers. What'da ya need?"

"Uh, yes, Detective Rogers, this is Sam Logan. You gave me your business card when I was assaulted in my tattoo shop a while back. You told me to call if I ever saw the guy again."

"Oh yeah," he replied, his tone casual, "you're that little dark-haired gal with all the tattoos on your body. Yeah, I think I remember you. How are you, did you heal up okay?"

Wow, Sam thought, shaking her head. *This guy's got the memory of a goldfish.*

"Uh, yeah… anyway, I found him."

"You found who, Ms.…?"

"Ms. *Logan.* The tattooed woman, *me.* The one who got assaulted. You guys never caught the guy."

"Oh yeah, right. The little tattooed girl." He chuckled. "Hey, does it hurt, you know, getting all those tattoos… everywhere?"

Sam sighed, already regretting the call. "I wouldn't know. I *don't* have tattoos everywhere. Can we focus on *why* I called, please?"

"Sure, sure. Uh, Ms. Logan, where'd you see the perp? Did he show up at your house or something?"

"No. I saw him walking down the street earlier when I was picking up groceries at Nguyen's Corner Market, over in the uptown area. I followed him back to his building. I don't know what room he's in, but how many bald guys have a pair of bat wings tattooed on the back of their head?"

"Honey, you'd be surprised. You got any bat wings tattooed on *you*?"

Sam took a deep breath. "No. But *he* does."

She gave him the cross-streets and the name of the rundown motel.

Rogers scribbled it down. "Alright. Anything else we should know?"

"Just this, when are you going to pick him up? I want to be at the station when you bring him in. I want him to *see* my face when you lock his sorry ass up."

"We'll see. I'll check in with the patrol sergeant and see when they can send a car down, if he's still there."

"Then you should *hurry*, while he's still there. I saw him less than an hour ago."

"Yes, ma'am. Like I said, I'll call the sergeant, get a car rolling."

"And call me when you bring him in," Sam added sharply. Her voice had an edge now.

"I'll see. We'll be in touch, Ms. Logan. Bye-bye now."

Click.

Sam set the phone down, rubbing her temple. A headache was already forming behind her eyes.

"Jimany Cricket," she muttered. "I'd have better luck getting Barney Fife to pick the guy up."

Sam took a couple of aspirin with a sip of her green tea.

"They'd better not let this guy slip away," she muttered. "Who knows where else he hangs out?"

She returned to her dinner prep and finally got everything finished. Pouring herself a bowl of soup, she grabbed her green tea and sat cross-legged at her drawing table. As she ate, she rifled through a stack of her old tattoo designs.

"Good... not so good... blah, trash... good," she said, tossing the rejects into the trash can and placing the so-so sketches in their own pile beside the good ones.

She was halfway through the bowl when she paused, her fingers had landed on a strange design.

It was a dragon… or maybe a serpent. Large, fierce-looking, with sharp horns and a glowing red crest on its forehead. The lines were intense, almost fevered in detail.

"Where'd this come from?" she said aloud.

It didn't look like her work. Not her line weight, not her ink style. And it definitely wasn't a photocopy or a reference sheet from a book.

She flipped through the rest of the stack again. That one drawing stood out, utterly unlike the others.

"Maybe Julie did it," Sam said, narrowing her eyes. "Maybe I grabbed it by mistake from the shop."

She set it aside in a neat stack with a mental note to ask Julie about it in the morning.

Once her soup was finished, she cleaned up the kitchen and carefully tucked Julie's vegan version into the fridge. She wandered back to her drawing table, pulled out a fresh sheet of paper, and started sketching ideas for her new tattoo. Her heritage tattoo.

At first, she considered the usual imagery: an American traditional headdress, an animal totem, maybe a portrait-style woman. But nothing felt quite right. Instead, she let her mind drift, let her hand guide itself.

And it did. Like it was tracing something already etched beneath the surface of the page.

She didn't force it. She just followed the rhythm of the pencil. Her strokes were softer, slower, deliberate but free.

Eventually, the hand stopped.

The image on the page didn't follow any particular tattoo style. It was old-looking, unfamiliar, like it belonged to some ancient tradition she couldn't quite place.

"It's... beautiful," Sam whispered.

She stared at it in awe. The design radiated something beyond aesthetic appeal, it felt *right*, like it had always been meant for her.

"This is the one," she said. "This is the tattoo I want. And I know exactly where to place it."

She gently placed the drawing in her drawer, laid a clean sheet of paper over it, and closed it with a soft tap of her fingers.

"You stay right there till it's time to ink," she said.

Her mind drifted back to the detective.

"I wonder if Detective Doofus found the guy yet," she mumbled. "No call probably means either A) he never even called the sergeant, or B) they picked him up and forgot to let me know."

She rolled her eyes. "Neither would surprise me."

It was getting late, but Sam wasn't ready to sleep. Not yet. She figured she'd rest eventually, but it wouldn't be for long.

Heading to the bathroom, she ran herself a hot bath, adding a dash of mint oil to the water. She stripped down and sank into the tub.

"Ahhhhh," she sighed, melting into the warmth. "I definitely needed this."

The apartment fell quiet. Still. Peaceful.

Sam closed her eyes and let the heat soak into her bones. For a while, the world drifted away.

Sam opened her eyes.

But she was no longer in the tub of warm water in her apartment.

She was sitting, naked and damp, in a dry, cracked porcelain tub inside *the old house*. The same house from her dreams. The same house with the party streamers, the birthday cake, the quiet that pressed in like fog.

Her skin broke out in goosebumps.

Sam stood up slowly, clutching the edge of the tub for balance, and stepped out. Everything was exactly the same: the decor, the rooms, the stifling air, the hollow stillness. A house dressed for joy but stripped of warmth.

She wandered through it, tense and watchful. She passed the dining room. The den.

Empty.

No shadow in the corner this time. No movement. No sign of *him*.

"I know you're here," she said aloud. "You can't hide. This hide-and-seek game is getting old."

A voice, smooth as silk and sharp as a blade, replied, close and distant all at once.

"Ah, Rebekka. Too old for games, are we? *My, how you've changed.*"

She stopped walking.

"Changed? Changed from what?" she said, her patience cracking. "What are you even talking about?"

As usual, the voice didn't answer directly. It never did.

"I still don't know who you are or what you want from me," Sam snapped. "I'm starting to think you're not even real. Just some figment, some hallucination. I need proof you're real!"

There was a pause.

Then, laughter, low, guttural, and growing. It filled the house like smoke, seeping through the walls, rattling the windows.

"*Proof?*" the voice purred. "You want proof? Oh, dear, dear Rebekka... You *shall* have proof. Just remember, you are the one who asked."

Something in the tone shifted. Darker. Sinister.

Sam's mouth opened to protest. "Wait, wait, I…"

She blinked.

146

And she was back.

She was back in her apartment's bathroom, in the bathtub, but the water was no longer warm. It was *ice-cold*. Bone-deep cold.

Gasping, Sam scrambled out, grabbing a towel as her teeth chattered. She stepped onto the floor and froze.

The water in the tub behind her... was no longer clear.

It had turned a faint rose hue. Red tint swirling through it.

She stared, paralyzed for a moment.

Then she pulled the drain and sat heavily on the closed lid of the toilet, wrapping the towel tighter around her shivering body.

Her fingers weren't wrinkled. Neither were her toes. She couldn't have been in the water long, but there was dirt beneath her nails. Dirt between her wet toes.

She blinked hard.

"What is this?" she whispered. Then louder. "What did you make me do?! *What did you do?*"

Her knees buckled, and she sank to the cold floor.

Face in her hands. A low sob escaped her lips, quiet and trembling.

"What did you do…" she murmured again, rocking slightly, alone in the silence.

Sam gathered herself and stood up, wiping her face with the edge of the towel. She tried to dry off, but her hands were still trembling. Slowly, she turned to look back at the tub.

The rose-colored water was nearly gone now, spiraling down the drain, and in its wake, clumps of dirt and mud were left behind, pooling like something dredged up from a grave.

Sam felt her stomach lurch.

What did I unleash?

"Why did I ask for proof?" she whispered, her voice barely audible over the drip of the faucet. "Why?"

She had no idea what the voice had meant, "*you shall have proof*", but now she wished she'd never challenged it. If it were only a figment of her mind, then it couldn't do anything. But if it wasn't…

If it was *real*...

Her heart stopped for a beat.

"Julie," she whispered, eyes going wide. Her mind snapped to her best friend.

Had something happened to Julie?

"Oh God, no. *Please* God, don't let it have done something to Julie!"

Still wrapped in her damp towel, Sam bolted into the living room and grabbed her phone off the drawing table. Her fingers were cold, slick. She scrolled through contacts, found Julie's name, and hit "Call."

The line rang once.

Twice.

Three times.

"Come on, Julie... please answer."

Four rings.

"Umm... Sam?" Julie's groggy voice finally crackled through the speaker. "Wha, what is it? Something wrong? It's like... three in the morning. Are... are you okay?"

Sam collapsed into her comfy chair like her legs had given out.

"Oh, thank you," she whispered. "Thank you, thank you, *thank you.*"

"Sam? Are you at church or something?" Julie muttered, still half-asleep. "Are you drinking this late, or early? Honey, what's going on?"

"I'm sorry," Sam breathed. "I... I guess I had a nightmare or something. I didn't realize what time it was. I'm just, I'm sorry about yesterday too. I'll let you get back to sleep."

A pause. Then Julie's voice softened. "Okay, Sam. I'm alright. Just sleeping. I'm sorry too, about yesterday. We'll talk at the shop later, okay? *Go back to bed.* Love you, sweetie."

"Love you too."

Click.

The line went dead.

Sam just sat there in silence, still shivering. Still wrapped in the towel. Still uncertain whether what just happened was a dream... or something else.

Later That Morning

Sam awoke still slumped in the chair, the towel clinging damply to her skin. Her neck ached. Her back was stiff. Morning sunlight spilled in through the window, but it didn't bring warmth or comfort.

She no longer felt strong. She no longer felt in control. What did it do? she thought.

And more than anything, Sam just wanted to know, what had the voice done while she was gone?

Chapter 7 - Just Another Dead Perp

Detective Rogers arrived at the Grande Motel after a call from patrol. They'd found the suspect, the one he was supposed to bring in for felony assault on a young woman at a tattoo shop, dead.

Same as the homeless guy from a few days back.

Rogers ducked beneath the yellow crime scene tape, his shoes squelching in the muddy, unkempt ground behind the motel. The Grande was a dump, cheap rooms, drugs, and hourly guests. The kind of place the city pretended didn't exist.

The body still hung from a thick cedar branch, swaying gently in the morning breeze. The coroner hadn't arrived yet, so no one had moved it. A couple of uniformed officers were nearby, chatting casually about last night's ballgame like it wasn't a damn horror show in front of them.

Rogers circled the corpse.

The man had been stripped, not just of clothes but nearly of skin. Shredded, hanging in tatters. The top of his scalp had been sliced off and shoved into his mouth. His entire body was bloodless, the skin pale and waxy. No blood pooled below. Not a drop on the ground.

Like someone had drained him clean, and carried it away. No identifiable footprints. Not even the victim's.

How the hell did he get up in that tree? The guy had to be two hundred sixty, maybe two hundred seventy pounds. No ladder in sight. And there's no way one person did this.

Whatever happened here, it wasn't just a killing, it was a statement.

Rogers shook his head. The tire tracks in the lot were useless. The dirt was a tangle of overlapping prints from motel guests, johns, and junkies. Good luck pulling anything clean out of that chaos.

They'd need forensics, fingerprints, hair samples, anything they could lift off what was left of the body. And even then, there were no guarantees.

The victim wasn't a good guy, rap sheet a mile long, but still, this was beyond vengeance. Beyond human.

And now it was his problem.

"Murder. Great," Rogers muttered, flipping to a new page in his notebook. "Just what I needed. A homicide tied to a piece of trash no one wanted to find in the first place."

He sighed and scribbled details. At least he had one bit of good news: he wouldn't have to track the guy down for the assault charge.

Maybe he'd deliver it in person, to the tattooed girl. Cute little thing.

"Yeah... probably deserves to hear it face to face."

He finished up, nodding toward the uniforms.

"I'm done here. Nobody touches him until the M.E. arrives, *nobody*. Ron, when you get those prints developed, drop a set by my desk. Got it?"

"Got it, Rogers."

The detective headed back to his car, an '87 Buick Grand National that barked like a hellhound when it started up. He peeled away from the curb, tires spitting gravel, leaving the crime scene in his rearview.

***

155

Sam finally wandered through the back door of the shop around eleven a.m. She looked rough, eyes bloodshot, hair a mess, shoulders slumped. She didn't even make it to her drawing table. Instead, she slumped into the small table in the back, the one reserved for late dinners or coffee breaks. She dropped a half-drunk green tea beside a Tupperware container of her garlic chili noodle soup, today's version meatless, just for Julie.

She didn't want to be here. But she *had* to see Julie. In person.

"Wow, girl... I hate to say it, but you look like hell," Julie said, stepping into the back. "Did you sleep at all? You sounded freaked out last night, well, early this morning. You okay?"

Sam looked up, eyes puffy and rimmed in red. "Julie, I feel like crap that's been run through a strainer. I may have got two hours of sleep, in my chair, wearing nothing but a towel. I fell asleep wet after a soak. Don't ask me. I think... I think I had a nightmare."

She slumped forward, resting her forehead on the table.

"I made my garlic chili noodle soup last night. No chicken this time. Special, just for you," she muttered.

Julie crossed her arms, concern heavy on her face. "Sam, honey... go home. I mean that in the nicest way possible. You need rest."

Sam's head snapped up. "*No.* I'm not going home. I want to be here. Please... don't make me leave."

There was something in her voice, raw, pleading. Her eyes held that vulnerable, frightened-little-girl look Julie had only seen once before.

"Okay, okay," Julie said gently, her voice softening. "We've got the old tattoo chair in the storeroom. I'll grab a blanket and pillow from my station. You can crash back here. I'll cover the shop."

Julie made quick work of setting up the chair, laying it out flat. Sam crawled on top without a word, pulled the blanket over her, and within minutes, she was out cold. Julie tucked the tea and soup into the fridge, then stood for a moment, watching her friend sleep.

157

She must've had one hell of a dream.

Julie was chatting with a couple of customers in the front as they were leaving. Julie turned to go to the back when the chime above the door jingled. She called over her shoulder, "I'll be right with you, feel free to flip through the design books!"

"That's fine. I'll just sit over here and wait," came a man's voice.

Julie turned, immediately recognizing him. "Oh, you're the officer who came by after Sam was assaulted, right? Bob Rogers?"

"Uh, Buk. Buk Rogers. Like Buck Rogers, but spelled differently."

"Right, right. Buck Rogers... twenty-fifth century or whatever."

He smiled politely. "Is Sam in today? I need to speak with her about her case."

Julie hesitated. "She's here... but she's resting in the back. Had a rough night."

Rogers raised an eyebrow, pulling out a small notepad. "Rough how?"

"She called me around three in the morning, sounded scared. Said she had a nightmare.

Something about thinking something happened to me. I was half asleep, but that's what I remember."

"Hello, Detective." Sam's voice came from behind the curtain. She stepped through, blanket still draped around her shoulders. "It's okay, Jules. I'm awake now. Think your voice woke me."

Julie smiled. "Oops."

Sam turned to Rogers. "What is it you needed to tell me, Detective?"

"Good afternoon, Ms. Logan. Is there somewhere private we can talk?"

"It's fine. Julie knows everything. She was with me when I was interviewed in the hospital."

"You sure?"

"I'm sure."

Rogers nodded. "Alright. The patrol unit rolled out this morning to arrest the suspect. The motel owner showed them the room, clothes were there, but he wasn't. Officers searched the property and... well, they found him. Out back. Hanging from a tree."

Sam's breath hitched. Not out of sympathy, *the voice said it would give proof.* Her blood ran cold.

"In a tree?" she repeated, masking her panic. "I thought you'd say he was hiding or something, not dead."

"No sympathy?" Rogers asked, scribbling in his pad.

"None," Sam said flatly. "Guy beat me senseless. Good riddance. How'd he die, OD?"

Rogers paused. "Can't share much, open case, but... it was a homicide. Cult-like. Real nasty stuff."

He looked up from his notes and down at Sam's tattoos, his gaze lingering.

Sam cleared her throat loudly. His eyes snapped back up.

"Where were you between midnight and five a.m.?" he asked, tone suddenly official.

Sam's brow furrowed. "You think I did this? You serious?"

"Just doing my job, Ms. Logan."

"I was at home. In the bath. I had a bad day, needed to unwind. Ask Julie."

Julie stepped in. "She did. She called me in the middle of the night. She was shaken."

Rogers raised an eyebrow. "So you two have some kind of lovers 'spat?" Julie and Sam both rolled their eyes.

"No," Sam snapped. "We're friends. Straight friends. And whatever we argued about has *nothing* to do with that guy being murdered."

"I was home," she continued. "Didn't leave till ten this morning."

Rogers jotted that down. "Got it." He slid the notebook back into his coat.

"Well, I appreciate your cooperation. Unless something new comes up, this case is closed. Perp's dead, and that ends it."

"Shame he didn't rot in a cell," Sam muttered. "But I'll take it."

The detective stepped forward and shook Sam's hand, his eyes flicking once more to her arm tattoos. Then to Julie's, as he shook hers.

"Those gotta hurt, huh?"

"Not as much as your questions," Julie said under her breath.

"Alright, ladies. You take care." He tipped an invisible hat and walked out, heading down the sidewalk to his car.

Once the door chimed shut behind him, Julie turned to Sam and wrapped her in a long, firm hug.

They stood there a moment, then both burst out laughing. After the laughter faded, Sam turned to Julie. The smile was gone from her face.

"Jules... I need to talk to you. Really talk to you."

Julie didn't look shocked, concerned, maybe, but she waved it off gently. "You don't have to, honey. I already forgave you for snapping yesterday."

"It's not about that," Sam said, her tone shifting. "It's something else. Something... more."

Her expression was dead serious. Julie's heart sank.

"We need to lock up for a bit. Say we're closed for lunch. I need to talk where no one can hear us. No one walking by, no one peeking in."

Julie's stomach dropped. *What the hell is this?* Was Sam using again? Was she about to bail on the business? Her mind spun with worst-case scenarios.

Without saying a word, Julie walked to the front of the shop, flipped the sign to *Out to Lunch – Be Back Later*, and locked the door.

Sam was already sitting at the small table in the back when Julie returned through the curtain. She approached slowly, her face uncertain.

"Okay…" she said carefully. "You're scaring me a little. Are you leaving the shop or something? Are you … " She stopped herself, held up her hands. "No. Never mind. I talk too much sometimes. Go ahead, Sam. What's going on?"

Julie sat and leaned in, placing her hands on the table, bracing herself.

Sam looked down, took a deep breath. "I don't even know how to start. I feel… ashamed. I've been lying to you, Jules. For a while now. I'm sorry. So sorry. I didn't know how to tell you. I didn't want to freak you out."

Julie stayed calm. Her voice was soft. "What kind of lies, Sam?"

163

Her eyes held no judgment, just open concern.

"After the attack," Sam began, voice barely above a whisper, "I started hiding. You probably guessed that. But it was worse than I let on. I was afraid to go out, afraid to be here, terrified every new client would be *him* or someone worse. I didn't feel like myself. And if I wasn't me… I didn't think I needed to *be* here anymore."

Sam's voice cracked. "That's… that's why I tried to kill myself."

Julie's face crumpled with quiet heartbreak. "Oh, Sam… my sweet Sam. I know. I *knew.* I gave you space, all the time you needed. I hoped you'd reach out, but, "

Sam gently touched her fingers to Julie's lips. "That's not all, Jules. I wish it were."

Julie blinked, confused.

"After the overdose… something changed. I started having dreams. You remember how I told you I hadn't dreamed in eighteen years?"

Julie nodded, slowly.

"These weren't normal dreams. They felt… guided. Like I was being pulled somewhere. At first, it was just a dark room. Then I heard a voice. It wasn't threatening. It was calm. Comforting, even. I wasn't scared, not then. And then it started showing me things... drawings I had to make."

Julie's brow furrowed, but she didn't speak. Sam needed to get it all out.

"I drew something in one of the dreams. It looked ancient, like an old symbol or creature. It was a dragon, maybe. Or a serpent. Two legs, scaled body, and a human-looking face, but wrong. Like a bad copy. Like... like a shapeshifter that didn't quite pull it off."

Julie's face stayed still, eyes wide.

"That's when I started lying again," Sam continued. "I didn't want you to know. I was scared, yeah, but not enough to stop. The dreams kept coming, and they got darker. The voice got stronger. I didn't fight it. I don't know why, but... I didn't want to."

Her hands started to shake. Julie reached across the table and gently took them into her own.

Sam looked at their hands, at Julie's steady grip, and her voice came out like a dry whisper. "It started to feel like… it was inside me. Like it was *mine*. And I didn't know if I wanted it gone."

Julie held tighter. Her voice was barely audible. "Sam… what is it? What's in you?"

"I don't know," Sam said. "But it's not done with me."

"I felt like I was losing my mind," Sam said, her voice low. "Like I was slipping, losing my grip on reality. I started going to that internet café down the street, you know the one. I was searching for answers. For the voice. What it was, or what it could be. But I came up empty. Nothing."

Julie didn't speak. She just listened, eyes wide but steady.

"Not long after that…" Sam looked down at the table, hesitating. "That's when the homeless man was killed. Remember? After our night out."

Julie's breath caught in her throat. "Yeah…"

"I, I saw him that night," Sam admitted. "He asked me for money, but I didn't stop. I kept walking. Then he grabbed my shoulder and spun me around."

Julie gasped, her hands covering her mouth. Tears welled in her eyes.

"I think I screamed. I don't remember much after that. I guess I blacked out or something. Because the next thing I remember... I woke up in my bed. That's why I called you that morning. I didn't even remember sending you that text. I don't *think* I did. Did you notice anything weird about it?"

Julie stared off for a second, then pulled her phone from her pocket. She scrolled for a moment, then stopped. "You signed it *Rebekka*. Sam... you never sign your texts. And you never go by Rebekka."

Sam swallowed hard, nodding slowly. "Exactly."

Julie looked stunned, but she didn't interrupt. "Go ahead, Sam. I'm listening."

"I didn't know anything had happened to him until I got to the shop and we saw the news. I swear."

Sam deliberately didn't mention the dirt and blood under her fingernails. The scratches. That stayed locked away, for now.

167

"After that," she continued, "I called Dr. West. From the hospital. I know you hate shrinks after what the system put me through in foster care, but I didn't have anyone else. I needed someone to… dig through the garbage in my head. Someone to help me figure out what's calling me. Pull out whatever's been locked away."

She looked up. "I lied to you. I said I had interviews, or I was sick. But the truth is I've been hiding in internet cafés. At home. In therapy. My next appointment's tomorrow."

Julie reached out, her hand still warm, still holding on.

"She's already helped me some," Sam said. "I remembered a few things, small, but real. That's when I searched for info about my real family. My parents. My brother, Jason. And that's when I found out…"

She took a breath.

"My dad, he was full-blooded Native American. That explained a lot. Things I'd felt. Thoughts I'd had. Why I never felt totally here. That's why I was so excited the other day, Jules. And so hurt when you didn't feel it with me."

Julie's expression cracked. Her voice was quiet, raw. "Sam, I'm so grateful you trusted me enough to tell me this. And I meant what I said, ride or die. I'm not going anywhere. Ever. And listen… if it *was* you who… who killed that man? I wouldn't blame you. Not even a little. What he did was evil. He deserved worse."

Sam shook her head. "I don't remember anything about his death. Nothing. All I know is, I saw him on the street a few days ago. I followed him, got the location, and called that idiot detective. That's it."

Julie leaned back, shocked. "Are you crazy?! What if he saw you? What if he came after you again? He could've killed you!"

"I know," Sam said softly. "But it's done now. I can finally breathe."

Julie narrowed her eyes. "What about the voice? Did it say anything about *him*?"

"No," Sam answered. "Nothing. That's the part I can't shake. The voice never mentioned him. Not once."

Julie exhaled, tense.

"Dr. West and I both think it's just a figment," Sam added. "A hallucination. But I need answers. Hopefully, tomorrow I'll get some."

Julie reached forward, pressing her forehead to Sam's.

"I'm always going to be here for you, Sam. Never forget that. You hear me?"

"I hear you," Sam whispered with a small, tired smile. "So… are you gonna eat the meatless, vegan soup I made for you, or what?" The tension of the moment faded.

Julie grinned. "You *know* it. Let's eat."

They shared lunch. Julie complained it was so spicy it burned a hole in her stomach. Sam laughed, the first genuine laugh in days.

Later that afternoon, they flipped the sign back to *Open* and helped customers with tattoo designs and ideas. They worked like normal, but something between them had changed, deepened.

When they finally closed up at ten p.m., both women went home.

That night, for the first time in a long time, Sam slept peacefully.

No visions. No voices.

Just sleep.

But tomorrow would come. And with it… more truth.

Chapter 8 - Dr West's office - session 2

Across town, in a dimly lit office, Dr. West sat
hunched over her laptop, blue light casting shadows
across the tired lines of her face. The screen
displayed a string of search tabs; each one
connected to a piece of a puzzle she hadn't known
she'd be assembling when she first met Sam Logan.
Or, *Rebekka H. Logan*, as the records listed her.

She'd finally traced Sam's placement back to a
foster center, a home specifically for girls of Native
American heritage. That had surprised her. Most of
the other girls were full-blooded, but Sam,
according to what she'd found so far, was only half.
That detail alone didn't sit quite right. Why had she
been placed *there*?

Dr. West was concerned, deeply so. The *shadow
figure* that had surfaced during Sam's light
regression session was troubling. Imagery like that
often pointed to profound trauma, often at a very
young age. And while Sam's adult life was certainly
marked by tragedy, Dr. West had a feeling the real

damage had been done long before the attack at the tattoo parlor.

The records began to take shape. Appointments. Enrollment papers. Addresses. She finally unearthed the family's location: Chester, Connecticut, near Cedar Lake.

Nothing jumped out in the records from before Sam's ninth birthday. No flagged behavioral issues. No police reports. Her school performance had been steady, even above average up until she stopped attending school. There was no reason given for her absence, just no attendance. But some notes told a story of structure and strict rules, especially from the father.

Harry Logan. A full-blooded Native American man, tribe unknown. He had been extremely private. No unrelated children were allowed in the house. Sam and her brother, Jason, weren't allowed to visit friends' homes either. School was fine, Harry couldn't control that, but their home was his world, and his rules reigned.

He had continued to practice tribal ceremonies and rituals, though the records were vague on

174

details. No tribe was named. No mention of visiting elders or family beyond the nuclear unit.

Sam's mother, who went by her middle name, Elena, was described in notes as "quiet," "reserved," and "obedient." She didn't challenge her husband and rarely let Sam participate in home tasks, though she occasionally allowed minor chores. There were no medical red flags in the files, no chronic illnesses, no therapy records for the kids. At a glance, the family seemed ordinary.

Too ordinary.

But then came the record that stopped Dr. West cold.

A single word in Sam's foster intake file:

Missing.

Not "deceased." Not "car crash." Not "domestic violence." Just… *missing*.

Her heart ticked faster as she scanned the next set of records.

There had been a funeral. For all three: mother, father, and brother. But no cause of death was listed. No obituary details of the cause of death. No mention of a wake, no viewing, only old photos of the three. A date, a location, and a brief, unhelpful phrase: *"private service held."* There was mention of an Indian ritual to be performed after the funerals. That was it.

Dr. West leaned back in her chair, frowning. "Why would they list 'missing' in one record and a funeral in another?"

It didn't make sense.

She clicked back and forth between documents, looking for anything she might've missed, a coroner's report, a police file, a newspaper clipping. But there was nothing.

She tapped her pen against her desk, the sound loud in the otherwise silent room.

"I'll need to make a few calls first thing in the morning," she muttered. "Something about all this just doesn't line up."

She closed her laptop and stared at the dark screen. The reflection that stared back at her looked more tired than she remembered.

***

The next day was Sam's appointment with Dr. West.

Sam arrived early again for her appointment with Dr. West. She sat in the waiting area, fingers tapping restlessly on her knees. Her nerves buzzed beneath her skin. She'd taken Dr. West's advice and dressed how she normally would, jeans, her favorite worn tee, a few leather bracelets, but she also added a little makeup this time. Not for vanity, but to bring some life back into her tired, colorless face. She'd looked rough this morning and knew it.

"Would you like anything to drink? Or maybe a mint?" the receptionist asked, smiling as she gestured toward a glass bowl.

Sam gave a half-smile. "No thanks, I'm good." Truth was, her mouth was dry, cotton-mouth dry, but she didn't want to ask for water. It felt like she was being needy.

Just then, the office door opened. Dr. West stepped out, warm and professional in her charcoal slacks and blouse. She looked out over the waiting room, then smiled when she saw Sam.

"Morning, Sam. I'm glad you took my advice. You look comfortable, and I like the eyeliner. Come on back."

She glanced at her receptionist. "Please hold all calls. I'm not sure how long we'll go today. If we're still in session when lunch rolls around, go ahead and take your break and let the voicemail handle the phones."

Sam stood and followed her into the familiar office, but something was different. A scent floated faintly in the air. Cedar trees… and lake water. The two smells didn't belong together, yet they stirred something almost familiar in her chest. A flicker of memory? She shook it off.

"Let's talk a little before we start the regression," Dr. West said, motioning toward the tall, high-backed chairs across from each other. Sam sank into the plush upholstery. She liked these chairs, they made her feel held, without feeling trapped.

Dr. West mirrored her posture. "Sam, I just want to say again, your body art is beautiful. It's part of you. I'm happy to see you wearing what feels like *you.*"

Sam looked away, a little self-conscious. "Thanks. I guess I was nervous the first time.

Today, I thought I'd just... be myself. And no one in the building gave me any looks, if that's what you're wondering."

"Exactly," Dr. West said with a nod. "No one's watching. That judgment? It's in your head, built from years of trying to hide." She reached over and gave Sam's knee a soft, affirming tap.

Sam smiled a little. The kindness was getting easier to accept.

"Let's ease in slowly today," Dr. West said. "I'd like to ask you a few questions first, nothing deep, just a warm-up. Is that okay?"

"Yeah. Sure," Sam said. Her body had settled. Legs crossed, arms resting on the chair like she owned the room. Dr. West made a mental note of the shift. A breakthrough, maybe.

"Tell me about life before your ninth birthday," Dr. West said gently. "Anything about your mother, your father, your brother Jason. How did they treat you? What do you remember, good or bad?"

Sam stared out the tall office window toward the fountain angel, the one with water cupped in its hands. The ripples were slow today.

"I remember being loved," she said. "But there were strict rules. Real strict. No guests unless they were blood relatives. One time, my dad's truck wouldn't start, and his coworker came to pick him up. But I don't think the man even came inside."

Sam paused, chewing her lip.

"My mom was quiet. Never spoke up much. But I liked her. I helped her with chores sometimes. Not all the time. She told me that Daddy didn't want me doing them too often, said I was *made for something greater.* I never knew what that meant. I still don't."

She glanced at Dr. West. "It wasn't creepy. Just… cryptic."

"And Jason?" Dr. West asked softly.

"He was little. Too young for chores. Mostly played in his room."

Dr. West leaned in slightly. "Anything else stand out?"

Sam's brow furrowed. Then she nodded slowly. "Yeah, one thing. Might seem weird now, but it didn't then. My father made me take a bath every night. No exceptions. Even if I wasn't dirty. He said

180

it was about 'cleansing. 'I don't know why. It wasn't about puberty, I was too young. Just... something he believed in, I guess."

She sighed. "Back then, it felt... normal. School, home. Rules. It was just life. Nothing strange, *to me* anyway."

Dr. West gave a slow nod, filing it away. "Thank you, Sam. That's what I needed. Just to feel out the landscape before the storm."

Sam gave a lopsided shrug. "If it's a storm, it's already raining."

Dr. West stood and motioned toward the couch. "Then let's get into the eye of it. Lie down. Get comfortable. We're going to go a little deeper this time, into those earlier layers, see what else lives down there. Maybe even meet your shadow man again... or find out where he's hiding."

Sam stood and stretched, then made her way to the couch. She pulled the blanket up over her legs and let out a long, slow breath.

She closed her eyes.

The air shifted. The scent of cedar deepened. The sounds from the fountain outside disappeared.

And slowly, the descent began.

Dr. West reached over and pulled out a small black device, placing it gently on the table next to her. It had no screen, just a few blinking lights and a volume dial.

"Sam, this device mimics environmental soundscapes, forest, beaches, cities, anything really. For today, I've programmed it with sounds from a lakeside setting: birds, water lapping, wind through the trees. Simple, familiar things. They help the mind reconnect to memories it's buried. Are you comfortable with that?"

Sam, eyes closed as she lay back on the couch, nodded slowly. "Yeah… that's fine."

"Good," Dr. West said, her tone soft but steady. "Let's begin."

She guided Sam through a slow, deliberate relaxation sequence, starting at the feet and moving upward. Each part of Sam's body was named and released, from toes to ankles, up through her hips and spine, chest, arms, neck, and finally her jaw and brow.

Sam's breathing grew deeper, slower, rhythmically in sync with the subtle sound of waves lapping on a distant shore.

"Sam, this is Dr. West. If you can still hear me, raise your index finger."

Sam's right finger lifted briefly into the air, then relaxed.

"Good. Very good. There's a projector beside you, Sam. Can you see it?"

Another lift and drop of the finger.

"Now, go ahead and start the projector. Let it run backwards, past the present, past your twenties, through your teenage years. It's still going... slowing now... slowing... until you see your six-year-old self. When you see her, stop the reel. Let me know."

Sam lifted her finger again, then let it drop.

"Excellent, Sam. The projector has stopped. Tell me what you see. What is six-year-old Sam doing?"

Sam's voice came out soft, dreamy, barely above a whisper. "I'm... in Jason's room. He's one today. He keeps grabbing my hair. He thinks it's funny."

A faint smile played across Sam's lips. She gave a quiet laugh, almost childlike.

Dr. West made a note in her pad. "That's very good, Sam. And where are your parents right now?"

"They're outside… making a fire in the circle."

Dr. West's brow furrowed slightly. "A fire in the circle?"

"Yes. Daddy is cooking today. He took down a big deer… for Jason's birthday. It's a celebration."

More notes.

"Is anyone else there? Or is it just your family?"

"No one yet. Uncle and Aunt are coming. With cousins."

Dr. West nodded, then reached over and switched on the sound machine. Gentle waves, tree frogs, and a breeze moving through tall grass began to hum softly through the room.

"Alright, Sam… let's move forward. You're now seven years old. Just watch. Just observe. Do you see yourself?"

A slight nod. Sam's finger lifted, then dropped.

"Where are you now, Sam?"

"I'm helping Mommy clean. Scrubbing the floors. Jason's napping."

"And your father? Where is he?"

Sam shifted slightly on the couch, her hands twitching beneath the blanket.

"He's… out back. Near the lake. He's dancing… around the fire."

"Dancing?" Dr. West asked calmly, pen poised. "Can you describe it?"

"He's going up and down… waving long sticks. Feathers tied to them. He's singing, but not in English. It's… something else. It sounds like an old language."

Dr. West underlined a note. "And the fire? Is he touching it?"

"No… he moves around it. Fast. Then slow. Back and forth. It's not a game, though. It's something else."

"What did your mother say about this? Does she know he does this?"

"Yes. She told me not to look when Daddy dances in the fire."

"Why, Sam?"

A long pause. Sam's breathing slowed again, like she was sinking deeper.

"Mommy said... *things* come out of the fire. Bad things. If I look too long, they might see me."

Dr. West stopped writing.

Her voice lowered, careful and quiet.

"Did you ever see them, Sam?"

Sam's head turned slightly on the pillow, but she didn't speak.

Her lips parted like she was about to say something, but nothing came out.

Dr. West leaned forward, watching closely.

"Sam... did you see something in the fire?"

Sam's voice dropped to a whisper so faint, Dr. West had to lean in to hear it.

"... yes."

"Don't tell Mommy," Sam whispered.

Dr. West leaned closer. The voice was faint, almost inaudible. "Sam, remember, you're only observing. Can you still hear me? If you can, raise your index finger."

Sam's finger rose, then fell.

"Very good, Sam. Now, what did you see in the fire? Can you describe it?"

"…No," Sam breathed. "They might hear me…"

She turned her head away from Dr. West, curling slightly on the couch.

"Sam, repeat after me: '*I am an observer. Nothing can hear me. Nothing can get me.*' Can you do that?"

"I am an observer. Nothing can hear me. Nothing can get me."

"Very good, Sam. You're safe. No one can hear you."

Dr. West steadied her voice. "Now, what did the thing in the fire look like?"

Sam's lips trembled as she whispered, "Black dancing smoke… with red eyes. It danced next to Daddy."

Dr. West's pen scratched hurriedly across her notepad. "Did it see you, Sam? Did you make eye contact with it?"

"With red eyes," Sam echoed softly. "Yes. It saw me looking. I ran to Jason's room."

Dr. West steadied her breath. "Did your mommy or daddy see it?"

Sam shook her head slowly. "No. I don't think so."

"Alright, Sam. Let's move forward now. Let's go to when you were eight years old, about a week after your birthday. Do you see yourself?"

"Yes," Sam said aloud this time. "I see her."

Dr. West raised an eyebrow, noting the switch in language. "What is eight-year-old Sam doing?"

"She's sitting. I'm sitting. In my bedroom. On the floor."

Dr. West frowned, scribbling quickly. Sam was now shifting between third and first person. A subtle fracture in identity.

"And where are your parents and Jason?"

"Yes… we see them. Mommy is in the kitchen. She's in the kitchen. Daddy is at work. He's at work. Jason is napping. *Tasty brother is taking a nap.*"

Dr. West's breath caught.

Tasty? That wasn't a child's slip. That was something else.

She covered her mouth with her hand, careful not to make a sound that might disrupt Sam's trance.

"Sam," she said carefully. "Why are you in your room alone?"

"I'm bad," Sam murmured. "She'ssss bad."

"Why are you bad, Sam? Is someone with you in the room?"

A long pause.

"I have a new friend," Sam said, giggling lightly. The voice was younger. Too young.

"I'm not supposed to have friends. My friend is here now."

Dr. West steadied herself.

"Sam, who is your friend? Can you describe them?"

"Dancing black smoke. With red eyes. He's my friend. We play together."

Dr. West's stomach turned. She hesitated, pen shaking slightly above the page. Should she stop the session? Push further?

I need to get to the bottom of this, she thought. *I have to find out what happened to her family.*

"Sam, let's move forward again. Two weeks after your ninth birthday. Can you do that? Raise your finger if you can."

No movement.

"Sam, this is Dr. West. Move your finger if you can hear me."

Sam's breathing hitched. Not enough to warrant ending the session, but enough to concern her.

"Sam... move your finger if you can still hear me."

Both of Sam's index fingers lifted, then dropped.

Dr. West's chest tightened. *That's new.*

"Sam, what is your nine-year-old self doing?"

"We are dancing. She is dancing. Around the fire... just like Daddy. Just like he did."

Dr. West leaned in. "And where are your mother, your father, Jason, do you see them?"

"No. We don't see them. She doesn't see them. They are no more."

A gasp caught in Dr. West's throat.

She didn't speak for a moment. Just listened. Sam's breathing remained slow. Rhythmic. Like she was deeply sedated.

Dr. West quietly moved to her desk and retrieved a stethoscope, pressing the chest piece to Sam's neck.

The pulse was sluggish, too slow. Almost unnatural.

She returned to her chair, voice calm but urgent now. "Sam... who is there with you?"

"My friend."

"Is your friend dancing with you around the fire?"

"Yes," Sam whispered.

"Where is your friend now?"

There was a long, dead silence.

Then, "Next to the projector."

Dr. West froze.

Her eyes darted to the floor beside the couch.

Nothing was there.

Still, her hands trembled.

"Alright, Sam. We're going to wake up now, okay? At the count of three, you'll wake up feeling rested, calm, and safe. Ready? One... two... three."

Sam's eyes fluttered, blinked slowly open. She glanced around the room, disoriented but calm. Her gaze landed on Dr. West, who gave her a tight but reassuring smile.

Sam smiled back. "Well... how did I do this time? Did you find anything out?"

Dr. West gathered her notepad, walked it to the desk, and set it down with a deliberate slowness. Her back remained to Sam as she leaned forward, hands braced on the desk's edge. Her silence was heavy, and the air between them thickened with the aftertaste of what had just transpired.

"Sam," she began, her voice quieter than usual. "I... I think I've found something, something key, in this session. But I'm not sure if I'm ready to tell you. And I'm not sure *you're* ready to hear it yet."

She turned around and faced Sam, who was still seated on the couch. Sam's posture was small, her fingers twisted tightly in her lap. Her face held a cautious blend of fear and hope. "What does that

mean, Doctor? Am I... sick? Am I losing my mind?
I don't understand."

Dr. West crossed the room and sat beside her.
The gravity in her expression made Sam's skin
crawl.

"Sam... let me consolidate everything we've
uncovered. There's research I need to do, things I
need to confirm. I need to make sure I understand
what we're dealing with before I say too much. I
don't believe you're in immediate danger, not to
yourself. But I *can't* say the same about anyone
around you."

Sam blinked. "Wait... what?"

Dr. West's tone softened, though her eyes
remained sharp. "I want you to go home, Sam. Stay
in, rest, don't push yourself. This isn't about
punishment or institutionalization. This is
precautionary. I want you to avoid emotional
extremes, anger, fear, grief. Anything that might
cause... a snap event."

Sam's voice cracked. "Are you saying I should
be committed? Am I going to hurt someone?"

"No. No commitment, no hospital, nothing like that," Dr. West said, taking her hand gently. "I just need time, twenty-four hours, maybe less, to figure this out. I'm not trying to scare you, but I *am* being honest. Something happened in that session. And it wasn't imaginary."

Sam's throat tightened, but she nodded, holding herself together.

"I'll stay calm," she said, voice trembling. "I won't get upset."

Her eyes welled with tears she refused to let fall.

"Is there anything I can do to help you, Dr. West? Research? Records? *Anything*, I'll do whatever it takes to get through this. To fix it."

Dr. West offered a bittersweet smile. "If something comes up, I'll call. I promise. I know you're strong, Sam. You've come this far."

Sam nodded again, swallowing hard.

She looked up, eyes pleading. "Just… answer me one thing?"

"Of course."

"Does this have to do with the shadow man?"

Dr. West hesitated. It was brief, but noticeable.

"Yes," she said at last. "Yes, it does."

Her gaze locked with Sam's. And in that moment, Sam could feel it, not just the doctor's eyes, but something deeper. Something *searching* behind them. It felt like Dr. West wasn't just looking *at* her... but *into* her.

And for a second... Sam wasn't sure she was the only one being seen.

Sam thanked Dr. West and stepped out of the office. She didn't hear the receptionist wish her a good rest of the day. She didn't hear the elevator ding or the traffic outside. Sam didn't hear much of anything.

The walk home was a bit of a hike, but it passed in a blur. Her legs moved on autopilot while her mind spun in tight, looping circles.

Is this what it feels like to lose your mind? Does she think I'm unstable?

Dr. West hadn't said the words out loud, but Sam could feel them between the lines. Maybe it was the way she said Sam should avoid others. Maybe it was the worry in her voice, the searching look in her eyes.

What if I have another personality? A second identity buried inside me?

The thought chilled her. What if the other version of her came out during extreme emotions, rage, terror, despair? Was that why she had to isolate? Was this *her*, or something *else*?

It had all started after the overdose, after she woke up in that hospital bed with a hole in her memory and a shadow hanging just behind her eyes. So many questions, and none with answers.

"I can't just sit around and wait," she muttered under her breath. It felt like she'd been put on a leash.

By the time Sam reached her apartment, she barely remembered the walk at all. She shut the door behind her, locked it with two turns, and leaned against the wood for a moment, eyes closed. The silence was heavy.

She paced the living room like a caged animal before cracking open the fridge and grabbing a cold green tea. Then she sat at her drawing table, opened her sketch pad, and pulled out the latest image.

She stared at it.

Is that me?

She didn't know anymore.

Chapter 9 - Fresno PD

Detective Rogers sat at his desk, flipping through the photos he'd been waiting for all morning. Crime scene shots from the tree victim. Nothing unusual, until something caught his eye.

"What the hell..." he muttered, holding one photo closer. There, in the branches above the deceased, was a single large feather. Probably a bird feather. Nothing unusual. And yet... it looked *off*. Too pristine. Too deliberately placed.

He flicked through the rest of the photos. Nineteen others.

The feather only appeared in one.

His brow furrowed. *Wait a minute...*

He opened the center drawer of his desk and dug through old files, papers, and case notes until he found what he was looking for, the earlier case. The homeless man. Same M.O., blood drained, skin torn.

Rogers flipped through those photos, heart rate ticking upward. There it was. Another feather.

Perched above the body in the branches, just like the other. He stared at both photos, side by side.

No one had noticed it back then. Not the first time.

But now it was screaming at him. He grabbed the prints and rushed down to the PD photographer's lab. "Hey, Ron," he called as he entered. "Can you blow these up for me? I want the feathers as clear as possible."

Ron took the photos, gave a quick nod. "Sure thing. You'll have 'em before the end of the day."

"Appreciate it." Rogers turned and headed back upstairs. His gut was talking now, and it wasn't saying anything good.

***

Back at Sam's apartment

Sam sank deeper into her oversized chair, wrapped in its plush comfort. She took a slow sip of green tea, then tilted her head back, resting it against the cushion. Her eyes drifted toward the kitchen, where her phone sat on the counter.

I need to call Julie...

But she couldn't bring herself to move. Not now.

"She'll understand," Sam whispered aloud. "I'll call her later tonight."

With a sigh, she closed her eyes, just for a moment. She didn't *mean* to fall asleep.

But she did.

The darkness returned, then gave way to light. Sam's eyes began to focus. She was back in her childhood home. She was about seven years old, standing in her mother's kitchen. Her mother was on the floor, scrubbing the wooden boards.

"Sam, would you hand me the other brush? This stain just isn't coming up."

"Okay, Mommy."

The observer, Sam's older self, watched as her younger self reached into the sink and pulled out a scrub brush.

"Here it is, Mommy," the little girl said, handing it over.

Her mother turned, placing her wet hands gently on the child's shoulders. "Now don't go looking out that window, Sam. You know you're not supposed to, especially if your daddy is doing some of his magic."

201

"Why not?" the child asked.

"Because the things that come out of the fire are very bad. Very, very bad, Sam. You don't want to see them."

"Yes, Mommy. I promise I won't look."

But the younger Sam peeked out the window, eyes wide, watching the black smoke dance in the fire while her father circled it.

"Don't look," older Sam whispered, a hand on her own forehead. "You promised."

Then, the child turned.

She looked straight at her older self.

"Rebekka," she said, "you promised not to look. And you broke it. Just for me."

But the voice wasn't that of a little girl. It was the voice of the smoke, of the shadow man. Smooth, sly, sarcastic.

Sam recoiled. Hearing that voice come from her seven-year-old self was wrong, unclean. She had been lulled into thinking this was a memory, something real and recoverable. But it wasn't. It was another vision. Another trap.

"Why would you bring me here?" she asked, her voice raw.

"To remind you, dear Rebekka. You wanted to find me, even when you didn't know it."

"Stop using her," Sam snapped. "Don't speak through her. It's disgusting. Go back to the smoke. Or the dark. Or whatever you really are. Just not her."

She turned toward the window.

From the yard, her father stopped dancing. He looked up. His face was calm, but when he spoke, it was the voice of the shadow again.

"He was not meant for me. It was always you, Rebekka. It's always been you. When I walked this land before man, I was meant to be with you."

Sam gripped the windowsill. The fear was crawling up her throat again, but she had to ask.

"What are you?"

She didn't expect an answer. The thing rarely gave one.

But this time it did.

"I was called the Uktena, by your people. Ulunsuti, by others."

203

I'm as old as time itself. I've always been drawn to you, Rebekka. You and I are meant to rule this world, and many others. You are the last. There are no more."

The voice moved like a serpent between the shadows, through her younger self, through the memory of her father, through everything.

"You are the gift. That's what draws me to you. Come. Be with me, Rebekka. Give yourself over to me."

Rule this world and others? What others? What gift?

Sam didn't understand. But the words burrowed in deep.

The Uktena.

A name she didn't know until now, but somehow it felt wrong.

A creature of myth. A great horned serpent, born during a time of chaos, when the spiritual and natural worlds collided. Created to punish those who broke the balance. Terrifying. Unstoppable. Only the rightful owner could command it. Everyone else would be consumed.

Then the vision shattered like glass.

Sam jolted awake in her oversized, worn-in chair. Her green tea had fallen to the floor. She blinked, disoriented. How long had she been out? The sun was low, bleeding orange and pink through her apartment blinds. Dazed, she got up, picked up the container, and shuffled into the kitchen. Her phone buzzed as she picked it up from the counter.

One missed call Dr. West.

* * *

At Dr. West's office:

Dr. West sat alone, phone still in her hand, anxiety heavy in her chest. She had already made several calls, colleagues she trusted, those with deeper experience in schizophrenia and dissociative identity disorder. What she'd seen in Sam wasn't unfamiliar... but it wasn't typical either. Not even close.

She described everything:
How Sam had referred to herself in both the first and third person.
How this other voice, this *presence*, manifested during regression.

How it had responded directly, interacted with her, even placed itself within the memory.

Her colleagues were intrigued, amazed even. Some wanted to fly out, see it for themselves. Dr. West shut that down immediately. Sam was not a lab rat. Not a case study.

She leaned back in her chair. Science had taken her far, but now it felt like she'd hit a wall. No diagnosis, no treatment path, no academic theory could explain what she'd witnessed.

There was only one name left on her list.

Raincloud.

A spiritual leader from one of the Oregon reservations. Some called him a medicine man. Others, a witch doctor. He spoke of spirit guides, energies, and ancestral visions, things far outside the reach of psychiatry. Dr. West had always been skeptical of that world. But she was out of options. If Raincloud couldn't give her something, *anything*, then she feared Sam might spend the rest of her life heavily medicated in a padded room. Not because she was dangerous. But because no one would know what else to do with her.

And Dr. West wasn't about to let that happen.

She stood and stretched. Her body was sore from hours of sitting, and her mind was just as worn. The twenty-four-hour deadline she'd given Sam was nearly up, and she still had nothing solid to offer. Nothing rational, nothing comforting. Nothing that could explain what was happening to the woman she had sworn to help.

She opened her office door and poked her head out. Her receptionist, her niece, really, her sister's daughter, was tidying up for the night.

"Sweetheart, can you find the number for that contact I told you about, Raincloud, the medicine man up in Oregon? He's the one from the reservation. Once you have it, call and transfer it to my office line, alright?"

Her niece nodded.

"After that, go on home. No use in both of us staying up all night. And tell your mom I'll make it over for coffee next week, I know I missed it this time. Work calls."

The young woman smiled and pulled out her little black address book, flipping pages with practiced speed. "Of course, Auntie."

Dr. West stepped back into her office and closed the door behind her, tension thick in the air. This was going to be an interesting call.

* * *

Across town, in the quiet back room of the shop, Julie glanced up at the old wall clock.

7:30 PM.

Still no word from Sam. Not a call, not a text. Nothing. It had been a good day, maybe the best day they'd had in weeks. A full roster of walk-ins, a dozen sketch requests, and even a few first-time piercings. Sam would've loved it. Julie picked up her phone, stared at the empty lock screen.

"Alright, Sam," she said aloud to herself, "you've got 'til ten o'clock. After that, I'm calling, awake or not." She set the phone down on the counter and returned to organizing the client sketches, her thoughts never far from her best friend.

Meanwhile, Sam was walking the cracked sidewalk under dim streetlights, heading toward the one place she thought might give her answers, the internet café. She knew that Dr. West didn't want her out and about, but this couldn't wait; she couldn't wait. She had its name now and an urgency to look into it.`

It was still open.

Thank God.

The glow of the monitors lit up the inside like a modern temple. Quiet. Half-full. Sam slid into her usual table near the back and handed cash to the guy behind the counter.

"Two hours this time," she said. "No cutoffs."

He handed her a slip with login info, and she wasted no time logging in.

She opened a blank tab, typed in the name the voice had given her:

Uktena.

She hit *search*.

She needed to know what it was. If it could be stopped. Bound. Banished. Anything.

Because if it had a name… then maybe, just maybe, it had a weakness.

Chapter 10 - Raincloud, Medicine Man

At Dr. West's Office

The line clicked, and a moment later, a low, smoky voice came through.

"Good evening, Dr. West."

"Good evening, Dr. Raincloud. I'm sorry to call at such a late hour, but I need your expertise with one of my clients."

"It's been a while," he said, his tone smooth and heavy, like gravel warmed by fire, so deep and steady it sounded like the kind of voice that had spoken to ghosts and gotten answers.

"It has," she admitted. "Too long, probably."

Dr. Raincloud didn't speak right away. Dr. West got the distinct impression he'd been expecting this call.

"You don't usually reach across the veil, Doctor. I assume this is serious," Raincloud said.

"It is," she said, and exhaled. "My client is of Native descent. The father was full-blooded, but I don't know which tribe. The mother was white. The

211

child, my client, was placed in a foster center after the rest of her family… disappeared."

"A spirit?" Raincloud asked, already ahead of her.

"I think so," Dr. West admitted. "But not in the traditional sense. I'm a scientist, Doctor Raincloud. A medical doctor. Psychiatry, trauma, dissociation, I know those worlds. But this… this is different."

"I assume you've seen signs?"

"Yes." She paused, unsure how much to say. "My client, during regression therapy, recalled a ritual their father performed when they were a child. Something about fire. My client saw something, black smoke, red eyes. They've been hearing a voice ever since. It speaks through memories, sometimes through their reflection. It calls them by a different name. Their real name."

Raincloud was silent. Then: "And you believe it possesses them?"

"Not completely. Not always," Dr West said. "Only during moments of intense emotion, fear, rage. I've seen personality switches before, but this… it isn't just trauma. It *knows* things."

"What kind of ritual?" he asked, his voice sharpening just slightly. "Do you know what was used? Feathers? Stones? Paints? Bones? Language?"

"I wish I had more," she confessed. "Everything I know was pulled through regression, fragmented memory. No photos. No artifacts. I don't even know what tribe to begin with."

She sat down, hand over her face. "I'm sorry. This may be a waste of your time. And mine."

There was a rustle on the other end of the line, paper maybe, or cloth. Then Raincloud's voice returned, calm but firm.

"Dr. West. I know you guard your patients' privacy fiercely. I respect that. But if you want to save her, I must insist... let me meet her."

Dr. West froze. He said she, as if he already knew.

"I... I can't make that decision lightly. You know how the system works, confidentiality, ethics."

"Ethics don't apply to the spirit world," Raincloud interrupted. "What is inside her is older

213

than any law you know. If it is what I suspect, and you do nothing, she will not last much longer. Neither will those around her."

Dr. West was quiet, unsure if her breath had caught from fear or awe.

"You already know the name, don't you?" Raincloud asked.

"…Uktena," she whispered.

"No…" Raincloud said, his voice tightening, laced with a subtle urgency. "That's what it *wants* you to think."

Dr. West felt a chill crawl along the back of her neck. "Then what is it, really? And why would it portray itself as another spirit?"

"*Skinwalker,*" he said. The word landed heavy, ancient. "Its entire existence is built on concealment, on deception. This spirit wants you to believe it's something older, something greater, something worthy of reverence or fear. But it's a liar. A mimic."

Dr. West swallowed, her mouth suddenly dry. "I've… I've heard of them. But only in stories. Folklore."

"They possess their victims when eye contact is made," Raincloud continued. "That's how it gains access. That's how it *entered her.*"

Dr. West gasped, heart racing. The memory of Sam, no, Rebekka, describing the red eyes in the fire, the moment their gazes met, flooded back.

"I was told long ago that I would hear that name again," Raincloud said, voice now lower, edged with something that might've been sorrow. "I hoped I never would. But now that I have... There is no time to waste."

***

FLASHBACK: THE VISION OF YOUNG RAINCLOUD

Somewhere in the High Desert, Years Ago

The air shimmered as young Raincloud walked alone across the high desert. He wasn't sure how he had gotten here, his feet had carried him while in a trance, his eyes wide but unseeing. His breath came slow, steady. Above him, three hawks circled, their cries sharp, insistent. They were his guides now.

The ground beneath him pulsed warm. The wind whispered in a language older than any man. He passed under an arch of bleached stone and stepped into a canyon none of the elders had ever mentioned. The sky above dimmed, though the sun still hung there. Everything felt dreamlike.

Then the hawks vanished. And the vision began.

The desert around him faded, replaced by *long ago*, a place buried in the memory of the land.

He saw a man standing tall on a stone outcrop, his body painted black with ash, eyes glazed with madness. A medicine man, once great, now twisted with ambition. The spirits around Raincloud murmured his name in a voice like wind through bones, in a language long forgotten: **Tse'nahgai**, "The Hollow One."

Raincloud watched as this man approached the tribal council, boasting of a great feat. He would become more than mortal, more than a spirit. He would *bind himself to eternity*, rising above even the ancestors.

The council was horrified. They saw it for what it was: blasphemy.

They *banished* him.

Raincloud's heart pounded as the vision carried him farther.

Tse'nahgai wandered the badlands, cutting his body, chanting in forgotten tongues, drawing ancient symbols in blood and ash. And something answered.

From the dark between stars, from the bones of the earth, a spirit older than his guides rose. It had no name Raincloud could understand, only a feeling: hunger.

The deal was struck.

Tse'nahgai offered his body, his soul, all that he was, and in return, the spirit would make him a *great spirit.*

But it lied.

It *merged* with him, twisted him into something monstrous. Skin tore, bones cracked, and his voice became a growl of many voices. He became the first *skinwalker*, a beast of rage and hunger, born not of ritual, but of corruption.

Raincloud gasped as the scene changed again.

Smoke and blood. Screams. The beast rampaged through its old village, killing those it once protected. The people fought back, warriors brave and terrified. In the end, they trapped it inside a cave and set it ablaze. The fire screamed. The beast died.

But the spirit did not.

Raincloud watched the flames flicker, and in them, something **moved**. It lingered. Waiting.

"Why am I seeing this?" Raincloud whispered.

A voice answered from all around him. It wasn't one of the hawks, but something deeper, slower. The spirit of the land itself.

"*Because you are the only one who can stop it from rising again.*"

"*It will take the form of a man once more. He will call the spirit up from the fire.*"

"*His name will be Logan, but not of the legend.*"

Raincloud trembled. "And what must I do?"

The wind paused. The earth fell silent.

"*You may sacrifice your life to save hers.*"

"Who?"

The answer came in the rustle of leaves, in the shadow of a young girl with a dragon tattoo not yet inked.

"You will know when the time comes."

Then the vision ended.

Raincloud collapsed onto the desert floor, sweat covering his brow. The hawks had returned, circling above once more, calm now. He was back in the waking world, but forever changed.

***

Back at the Cafe with Sam.

The search returned hundreds of results, images, folklore articles, tribal preservation sites. Most were broad or vague, but a few felt promising. Sam narrowed her eyes and clicked on one that read: *"Indian Mythological Creatures and Spirits."*

A page unfolded, cluttered with names that sounded half-familiar and wholly ominous: *Wendigo, Skinwalker, Chindi.*

She scrolled slowly, scanning descriptions and hand-drawn sketches. Emaciated beasts with ice in their hearts, shadowy tricksters wearing stolen faces, spirits of the unburied dead.

Then she saw it.

Uktena.

A stylized serpent curled across the screen, massive and coiled, horns on its head and scales shimmering like obsidian. A single blurb beside it read:

"A powerful spirit of the earth, a serpent, with a blazing crest upon its forehead. Feared and revered. Said to bring both vision and madness."

Sam leaned closer. "It's a serpent…" she murmured. "But the voice, what it shows me, it's smoke. Black smoke. Red eyes. Why would it hide behind a different shape?"

Her gut twisted.

She opened a second tab and began cross-referencing *Uktena* with "black smoke" and "red eyes." The results began to shift, pointing away from the Uktena and toward other entries. Misleading spirits. Tricksters. Impostors.

Then the word came up again and again:

Skinwalker.

Sam's breath caught in her throat. She clicked on one article.

"They wear the faces of what they are not. They

mimic. They deceive. They gain access through the eyes."

Sam sat back in her chair, fingers drumming nervously against the plastic desk. Her reflection in the blackened monitor beside her looked gaunt, pale. Her thoughts swirled.

This doesn't feel right. Uktena feels... off. Too clean. Too structured. Too mythic.
She glanced back at the twisting serpent image, now cartoonish against what she had *seen*, what she had *felt.*

Her stomach knotted. "Why lie?" she whispered. "What does it get out of pretending to be something it's not?"

No answers came. Just a growing weight in her chest.
She suddenly felt like she was being watched.

Sam shut the tabs, closed the browser, and reached for her tea bottle, empty.

She had more questions now than ever. And her gut kept repeating the same phrase, over and over:

You already looked once. You saw it. And it saw you.

Sam stood up from her table, picked up the empty green tea bottle, and walked it to the trash can. The hollow clunk echoed louder than it should have.

Her thoughts buzzed as she stepped back into the cool night air. *Why don't I believe it?* She wondered. *Why does everything it says feel like a mask, like it's playing a role?*

She couldn't stop the spiral in her mind. But somewhere inside the noise, a clear thread had begun to form. *I have to know. No more being dragged into these visions. If it wants to speak, fine. But this time... I call the meeting.*

By the time she reached her apartment, she barely remembered the walk. Her hands were already moving on instinct, door unlocked, then bolted shut behind her. No lights turned on. She didn't need them.

She walked straight to the kitchen, grabbed a glass from the shelf, and filled it with tap water. From there, she crossed into her bedroom, picked up the amber bottle from her nightstand.

Her fingers trembled just a little as she unscrewed the cap.

Sam took out a single pill, placed it on her tongue, and took two slow sips from the glass of water. Then she lay down, flat on her back, eyes open, and stared at the ceiling.

The quiet hummed around her. The shadows stretched. Her heartbeat slowed.

This time, I'm controlling the meeting, she thought, letting her eyes close.

Then she whispered aloud into the darkness: "Come find me, if you dare."

And the dark… answered.

The darkness enveloped Sam, pressing in from all sides like walls made of smoke. *This isn't real,* she reminded herself. *It's not a physical space. I'm in control.* She clenched her fists, grounding herself in the thought.

"Well, this is an unexpected visit, Rebekka," the voice murmured, drifting from the dark like a silk ribbon dipped in poison. It sounded almost… amused.

"Face me," Sam demanded. "Show me who you really are. You're not what you make yourself out to be."

"My, aren't we full of ourselves today?" it replied, condescending and sly.

"You better believe it." Sam forced steel into her voice, even though part of her still trembled. "Now, are you going to face me or not?"

A dim light sparked in the darkness, spreading until it revealed a full-length mirror standing in what looked like the corner of a room. Sam eyed it warily.

A mirror? Really? She smirked. "I don't plan to touch up my makeup for you."

"You will learn to respect me," the voice hissed. "I am the great Uktena, Rebekka."

"I might respect the *real* Uktena," Sam shot back, stepping closer to the mirror. "But you? I don't believe that's who you are. And if you were truly powerful, if you *were* some ancient spirit, you would've destroyed me by now."

Silence.

"Hello?" she said into the stillness. "Did I strike a nerve?"

She moved toward the mirror, uncertain but determined. The reflection that stared back wasn't quite right. It was *her*, but off, just slightly distorted in ways she couldn't name.

"Here we are, Rebekka... face to face," the voice whispered, low and cutting.

Sam stared at the image. "Nope. That's still me. I'm face to face with my *reflection*."

She narrowed her eyes, her voice sharpening. "You're a liar. You're *not* a Uktena. You're afraid to show me your real self."

The room began to quake. The mirror vibrated. A deep rumble stirred from the corners of the dream-space, and the reflection began to shift, elongating, twisting, unraveling. The lines of her face contorted, stretching into something strange and unusual. A low growl echoed from the walls.

That sound.

It seemed to rattle through her head. Familiar... but wrong.

Sam took a breath,

And jolted awake.

The bedroom was dim, gray-blue with streetlight bleeding through the blinds. Her heart thudded. Something rang in the distance.

The phone.

She sat up, slow and groggy, still under the pill's effects. Her limbs felt numb. Eventually, she was able to get off the bed and shuffle into the kitchen. Sam spotted her phone glowing on the counter.

Julie's wild, smiling face filled the caller ID screen.

Sam tapped to answer. "Yeah… hey, Julie. Sorry, I didn't call."

"Sam! What the heck, girl?" Julie's voice cracked with concern. "You had an appointment this morning, and then you *vanished*! I haven't heard hide nor hair from you all day."

Sam winced, rubbing her temple. "I know. I'm sorry, Jules. I got side-tracked, forgot to check in. The session… it messed with me. I stayed home. I've been stressed out since."

There was a pause on the line. Then Julie softened. "I forgive you, Sam. I just wanted to make sure you were okay, not lying in an alley somewhere."

"I'm not," Sam mumbled, finally starting to feel a little more awake. "I'm here. I'm okay. Just... exhausted."

"Okay," Julie said, but Sam could still hear the weight of worry. "Just... don't go radio silent on me again, alright?"

"I won't," Sam said. "Promise."

***

At Dr. West's Office

Raincloud's voice came through the receiver, low and grave.

"The skinwalker will continue to wear her down. It needs her to surrender. Once she gives up, gives *it* permission, it will fully possess her. Everyone around her will be in danger."

Dr. West swallowed hard. "And Sam? What happens to Sam?"

"Gone," Raincloud said without hesitation. "Your client, as you know her, will cease to exist.

The skinwalker doesn't share. It consumes. It will use her body until it's no longer useful, then it will jump into someone else. It leaves a trail of death and madness."

Dr. West pressed her hand to her forehead, her pulse pounding at her temples. "So what do we do, Raincloud? How much time do we have?" She exhaled, then asked the question that had been gnawing at her. "And... one more thing. I don't understand why it waited. It possessed her at seven, I'm sure of it. It did *something* to her parents. Then... nothing. It vanished, until she was older. Until... well, until something happened. Something I can't speak of."

Raincloud was quiet for a moment. Then, his voice sharpened.

"You said it went dormant? Like it went into hibernation?"

"Yes. For nearly two decades," she confirmed. "It entered her, *Rebekka*, when she was seven. It stayed with her until she was nine. That's when the incident with her family happened, her parents and younger brother vanished. Some say it was an accident. Some say it was murder. Officially, it's unresolved. But after that... the voice, the presence, it all went quiet."

"That's rare," Raincloud murmured. "Unnatural, even. Spirits don't sleep without reason."

Dr. West leaned forward in her chair. "So what does that mean?"

"It means something forced it into silence," he said, "or it willingly went dormant because it *had to wait*. I need to understand why. I will consult my spirit guides tonight. They will show me what is hidden."

"Raincloud..." Dr. West said, trying to steady herself, "We're running out of time. She's cracking."

"I know," he replied. "I'm booking a red-eye flight now. I'll be at your office by morning. Can you bring your client in?"

"I'll try," Dr. West said, her voice barely above a whisper. "I'll do whatever it takes."

"Good. We don't have long. And Doctor..."

"Yes?"

"Make no mistake. This isn't just a haunting or a possession. If what you've told me is true, then what resides inside that girl is *rare one*. And it's not finished."

***

Back in Sam's Apartment

As soon as Sam ended her call with Julie and placed the phone back down on the countertop, it rang again.

She blinked at the screen. *Dr. West.*

Sam picked it up and tapped answer.
"Hello, Dr. West?" Sam answering, questioning the lateness of the call.

"Hello, Sam." Dr. West said with a tiredness in her voice. "I know it's late, I'm sorry to bother you at this hour, but I've been working my contacts list since you left this morning, and… I think we've discovered what's been disrupting your life."

Sam exhaled slowly, her body still sluggish from the pill, but her mind sharpening.
"Oh… Dr. West, that's *amazing*. Please, please tell me we can finally get this thing *out* of my head."

A brief pause on the other end. Then:

"We *might* be able to. But I need something from you first."

Sam's stomach dropped.

"What is it?" she asked cautiously, her voice tightening. "What do I have to do?"

"I need you to come into my office in the morning. And I need you to meet someone. A contact of mine. I believe he can help, but he has to meet you in person."

Sam hesitated, glancing down at her feet. It was hard enough opening up to Dr. West, she wasn't sure she could bare her soul to a stranger, especially not another professional who might label her as unstable.

Dr. West continued, gently but firmly. "How do you feel about that? You don't *have* to, Sam. But I believe... It's in your best interest. *And* your friends'."

That last part made Sam freeze.

Julie...

Her heart climbed into her throat. "So it's not just about me anymore?" she said, her voice softer, almost flat.

"No," Dr. West replied. "It never really was."

Sam closed her eyes for a moment, centering herself. "Okay… if you put it that way, I don't really have a choice, do I?" She took a breath. "Can you at least tell me who this person is? And… how reliable they are?"

There was a long pause before Dr. West spoke again. "Sam… he's not a psychiatrist."

Sam blinked. "Then what is he?"

"He's a Native American medicine man." Dr. West responded.

There was a beat of silence. Sam nearly rolled her eyes, but stopped herself.

That actually… kind of makes sense, she thought. If what's inside her really *is* some kind of ancient spirit, then maybe this was the only kind of help that would work.

"Okay," she said finally. "Dr. West, I'm all in. Who is he?"

"His name is Raincloud. Dr. Raincloud. He's a medicine man from one of the Oregon reservations. Highly respected. He's helped people… when no one else could."

Sam nodded to herself. "What time should I be there?"

"Nine-thirty," Dr. West said. "Raincloud's arriving early, but just in case there are delays, that should give us a cushion."

"I'll be there," Sam said, trying to sound more confident than she felt. "See you then."

"Sam, one last thing," Dr. West added. "Stay calm tonight. And tomorrow morning. No intense emotions. We don't want to trigger *it*. Don't give it a chance to surface."

"Got it," Sam said, smirking faintly. "Zombified Sam. I can do that."

Dr. West chuckled softly. "Good. See you tomorrow."

"Goodnight, Dr. West."

As the line clicked off, Sam glanced at the time, **11:30**. Her body was tired, her brain buzzing.

***

Back at the Dr. West office

Over at Dr. West's office, the doctor set her phone down and leaned back in her chair.

She rubbed her temples, then glanced toward the leather couch in the corner of the office.

"Guess I'll be sleeping here tonight," she muttered.

She looked out her office window and stared at the angel fountain, water flowing from the angel's cupped hands. "God, if you're listening, can you help us tomorrow, please."

Tomorrow, everything might change.

Sam arrived at Dr. West's office early, like always.

She hadn't slept since their late-night call. She didn't want to sleep. She didn't want another vision. So she sat in the waiting area, staring at nothing, imagining, hoping, that maybe, finally, this nightmare could be coming to an end.

The office door opened.

Dr. West stood there, looking at Sam's sleep-deprived face with a mixture of concern and resolve. She gave a small, quiet nod, motioning for Sam to come in.

Sam took a breath, stood, and followed her inside, nervous but clinging to the hope that something might finally shift.

The moment she entered the room, Sam noticed him: an older man sitting in one of Dr. West's tall, comfortable chairs near the window. He stood as she walked in.

Sam hadn't known how to dress for this meeting.
Professional? Casual? Mysterious-spirit-banishing chic?

In the end, she chose comfort. Faded jeans with slashed knees. A sleeveless black tee. Her worn-in boots. A patchwork of tattoos visible across her arms and shoulders, framed by leather bands and bracelets.
No hiding. No pretense.

She'd even called Julie before leaving, offering just enough to keep her from worrying, but not enough to invite too many questions.

The old man stepped forward.

"I am Raincloud, of the Oregon reservations," he said, his voice like slow thunder. "You must be Rebekka."

He extended his hand. Sam hesitated, then took it, opening her mouth to correct him, but before she could speak, Raincloud placed his other hand gently behind her neck and closed his eyes.

Sam stiffened. She shot a glance at Dr. West, who stood still, watching carefully but not intervening.

Raincloud inhaled slowly, the skin of his brow tightening slightly as he concentrated, not just touching Sam, but *feeling* her, around her, through her. Searching. Sensing.

Then, quietly, he removed his hand and brought it to the leather pouch around his neck. His eyes stayed closed another moment. Then he stepped back, opened them, glanced at Dr. West, and gave her a small nod.

He sat down again.

Sam remained standing for another beat, confused and tense.

"Uh… hi, Mr. Raincloud," she said cautiously. "I'm Sam. I don't go by Rebekka. I'm sure Dr. West probably told you that already."

She glanced between the two of them, then crossed the room to the other high-backed chair and sat, never taking her eyes off Raincloud.

"So… what was that about?" she asked, trying to keep the edge out of her voice. "I'm kinda paranoid about people just touching me without asking, but I figure that must be part of your… diagnosis technique?"

Dr. West rolled her desk chair over, positioning herself near Sam.

"Sam," she said gently, "this session, if we can even call it that, won't be like our others. Dr. Raincloud isn't here for therapy in the traditional sense. He's here to sense the spirit. To understand it."

Dr. West paused, her voice soft but steady.

"He arrived early this morning to meet with you. To see if he can help, if he can get it out of you. This time belongs to him."

"May I call you Rebekka?" Raincloud asked gently, though his voice carried gravity. "I want to address you as you were named when the spirit entered you. I don't want separation between who you are now... and who you were then."

His eyes met hers and held, deep, unblinking. Searching. Sam felt it, like he wasn't just looking at her, but *into* her. Like he'd found a seat in the darkened room where the voice lived, and was just waiting for it to show itself.

"Uh... well, I guess that's fine. For this meeting," Sam said, her voice wavering slightly. "I don't want to hinder anything that could end this nightmare I seem to have been... cast into."

Raincloud raised an eyebrow, his gaze still locked with hers. "Cast into," he echoed. "That's an interesting choice of words. Why do you call it that?"

"I don't know... It's just a word I chose, I guess."

Sam glanced toward Dr. West, uncertain whether she was answering correctly, or if there *was* a correct answer.

Raincloud didn't blink.

"Who is it I'm speaking to now? The child who hides… or the spirit that has invaded her? You *will* tell me, spirit."

He reached up and gripped the small pouch around his neck, shaking it gently in Sam's direction. A soft rattle echoed between them.

Sam flinched.

Her stomach twisted. Something shifted. She could feel it now, the cold edges of the room, the dark one, curling in around her like smoke. Her breath caught.

Raincloud repeated the question, his voice sharper.

Sam opened her mouth to respond, but the words that came weren't hers.

"What do you want with me, medicine man?" the voice hissed through her lips.
"You have no authority here!"

Sam's eyes went wide, *inside*. Panic clawed at her chest. That, *that*, had never happened before.

Raincloud remained steady, calm, rooted.

"Why do you want this child?" he demanded. "Who called you into this world?"

Sam's head tilted back, eyes rolling white.

She was gone from the room.

Inside, she floated in the familiar dark, trapped again. She could hear them, faintly: Raincloud's voice, and the voice of the spirit.
Her voice, but not hers.

"Go away, medicine man," it spat. "This child belongs to me. Do you not know who you speak to? I am the great and powerful Uktena! I demand your respect!"

Dr. West sat frozen in her chair, jaw tight. This... this was beyond anything she'd ever seen. Even in her earlier work with Raincloud, she'd never witnessed a manifestation like this.

Raincloud stood his ground.

"You are no Uktena. You *mimic*. You *lie*."
His voice was firm but not angry, righteous without wrath.

"Tell me, spirit, what do you want with this child?"

Silence.

Only the soft sound of the water outside in the angel fountain, cupped in marble hands. A few distant cars hummed past on the street.

Then:

"She is mine, medicine man. She looked upon me as I danced, and she *invited* me in."
"Leave now… or I will end her."

"You speak lies," Raincloud said, unfazed. "You are a spirit of lies. You *cannot* end your host, if she dies, so do you."

"You think your medicine is strong. It is *weak*."
"I see your end, medicine man."

Sam's body remained rigid, her face blank, eyes still rolled back. Head tipped toward the ceiling like a puppet with snapped strings.

Raincloud stepped closer, placed one steady hand atop Sam's, the other gripping his pouch again.

"Rebekka," he said gently. "I know you can hear me."
His voice dropped, softened.

"Rebekka… open your eyes. See me. Come back now."

Sam twitched, once, then again.

241

She heard him, faint but growing clearer.

She felt the voice recoil, shrinking, like smoke retreating from fire. The darkness peeled back.

Her eyes fluttered.

Shapes returned. The office. Light. Raincloud.

She slumped back into the chair, her muscles releasing all at once. A limp weight again in her own body.

"Sam? Sam, can you hear me?"
Dr. West was crouched at Sam's side, holding her hand and gently patting it.

"I, I can hear you, Dr. West," Sam whispered, her voice hoarse and low.

"Oh, thank God," Dr. West sighed, her shoulders sagging. "You were unresponsive for a full minute. I thought we lost you for a bit there."

Sam blinked slowly, gathering herself. "No... I'm here. Just... glad I'm not in the dark anymore."

Dr. West nodded and gave her hand a final squeeze. "I'm going to let Dr. Raincloud continue now. Do you need anything? Water? Coffee?"

"No. No, I'm good." Sam sat up straighter in the chair, forcing her breathing to steady. Her eyes drifted back to Raincloud. "Just glad to not see the darkness."

Raincloud watched her, calm and unmoving. "Is… is that normal?" Sam asked. "That blackout? Everything went dark, just like the dreams. Like the visions."

"You may call me Raincloud," he said, soft but firm. "There is no 'normal 'with a spirit like this. What you're experiencing is the spirit's attempt to suppress you. It knows it's threatened. That's why it struck back."

He shifted slightly, his hands still gently resting on Sam's and on the small pouch around his neck.

"Dr. West told me how this began, how you saw it. Locked eyes with it as a child. That's how it entered. But Rebekka…"
His gaze sharpened.
"…how did you put it into hibernation when you were a child? Do you remember?"

Sam looked down, brow furrowed. "I don't know," she said quietly. "I don't ever remember it being inside me, not until recently. Everything I've learned came from the regression sessions. I remember my parents... my little brother... but nothing else."

She exhaled, rubbing her hands over her jeans. "The next thing I remember, I'm nine. A car shows up to take me to the foster center in Chester. No one told me what happened. No relatives took me in. No goodbyes. Just... silence."

Raincloud's brow furrowed deeply, eyes narrowing as he sat back in thought. He needed to connect the moment of possession with the time the spirit went dormant. Some *event* had locked the spirit away, but what?

"I understand from Dr. West that your parents were in some kind of accident," he said carefully. "Is that correct?"

Sam nodded slowly. "That's what the paperwork said, that's what I was told. Accident. But... even now, that just doesn't feel right. I don't *remember* anything like that. Just... blank. Like everything before, the car ride was cut away."

Raincloud exchanged a glance with Dr. West, who looked equally troubled.

"The records," Raincloud said, "were inconsistent. Dr. West told me that. Reports that contradicted one another. No clear cause. No clean story."

Sam's voice dropped to a whisper. "I always thought maybe… it was just a car crash or a fire….or they didn't want me anymore."

Raincloud shook his head solemnly. "No, Rebekka. Something happened. Something *broke* the spirit's control over you… long enough to bury it. And we must understand what that was. Because the key to *banishing* it… may be locked in that forgotten moment."

"Dr. West, we need to take Rebekka back, back to her nine-year-old self," Raincloud said. "That memory… It's the key. But the spirit will fight to keep us from finding it. It clouds the truth. We need to keep it at a distance."

Dr. West nodded slowly, considering. "We can use regression again, but that's a long process. It could take hours just to reach that depth. Is there a quicker path?"

Raincloud reached into the inside pocket of his jacket and drew out a small leather pouch. From it, he retrieved a capsule, the color of damp earth. Sam had never seen anything like it. Dr. West leaned forward cautiously.

"This," Raincloud said, "is peyote. Sacred medicine. It brings altered states of awareness, vision clarity. Normally, it's used with fasting, singing, prayer, and fire. But we don't have those here. And we don't have time."

He gently opened Sam's hand and placed the capsule in her palm.

Dr. West quietly excused herself, stepping out to retrieve a small cup of water. When she returned, she handed it to Sam with a steady hand.

Sam looked down at the capsule, her fingers trembling slightly. "Is this safe?" she asked. "I swore off drugs. I promised myself I'd never take anything again after... well, you know."

Raincloud met her eyes with quiet conviction. "This is not a white man's drug. It is sacred. Given for healing, not escape. I would never ask you to break a vow, Rebekka. But this… this may be your way out."

Dr. West placed a reassuring hand on Sam's shoulder. "It's safe. I trust him, Sam."

Sam looked between them, then down at the capsule. With a deep breath, she placed it on her tongue and washed it down with the water.

"Okay," she said, setting the cup aside. "Now what?"

Raincloud raised his hand and gently pressed a finger to her lips. "Shhh. Close your eyes. Sit back. Don't speak."

Sam leaned into the chair, exhaling slowly. Her nerves jittered beneath her skin, but she obeyed, letting the quiet fall over her.

Raincloud clutched the pouch around his neck and began to chant softly in a language Sam didn't recognize, low, rhythmic syllables, carried like smoke on the wind. The sound curled through the room like incense.

At first, Sam felt nothing. Then, slowly, her limbs relaxed. Her breathing deepened. Warmth filled her chest, and her mind began to drift. The room around her faded, and she heard only the gentle trickle of water, like a fountain. Peaceful.

Then she heard Raincloud's voice, far away but still close. A thread in the dark.

"Rebekka… Rebekka. Do you see her? Open your eyes and look upon the nine-year-old girl."

Sam's inner vision opened. She saw herself, smaller, younger, sitting cross-legged on her bedroom floor. Eyes closed. Meditating.

"Yes," Sam whispered. "She's there. I see her."

Raincloud's voice guided her like a current. "What else do you see, Rebekka? Is she alone?"

Sam's eyes, in the vision, drifted to the corner of the room. A shape lingered, vague, dark, shifting.

"There's… a smoky figure. In the corner. It has red eyes."

"Rebekka," Raincloud said gently but firmly, "look closer. Is it really smoke? Or is it something else, a man, perhaps?"

"No," Sam said. "It's smoke."

"Look closer, Rebekka. You must look. Who is it?"

"I… I'm afraid."

248

"Do not be afraid," Raincloud said. "There's a mirror in the room. Do you see it?"

Sam's gaze shifted. There, against the wall, stood a full-length mirror, its surface murky in the dim light.

"Yes," she said. "I see it."

"Then look into it," Raincloud said, voice quiet as thunder. "Look into the mirror. What do you see?"

Dr. West glanced at Raincloud, a furrow forming between her brows. Her mind churned, *How would he know there was a mirror in the room?* There had been no mention of one. Then realization struck her like a stone, *he's not seeing it, he's guiding her to see it. He's suggesting it... controlling the vision.*

"Rebekka," Raincloud said, voice low and even, "look at the corner of the room, but through the mirror's reflection. Tell me what you see."

Sam gasped, soft but sharp. "It's... my father. Daddy?" Her voice trembled. "No, why...?"

Tears trickled from the corners of her closed eyes.

"Rebekka," Raincloud said gently, "you're only an observer. Do not feel. Just watch."

Dr. West instinctively brought a hand over her mouth, her heart pounding. *Her father?* She hadn't expected this. None of this.

"Rebekka, what is your father doing there in the corner?"

Raincloud's grip tightened slightly around Sam's hand. The other clutched his pouch. He needed to keep the spirit away, just a little longer.

"He's saying something," Sam murmured. "Chanting. I don't understand it… But it's rhythmic. Like a prayer."

"Good. Now… look into his eyes. Through the mirror. Tell me the color of his eyes."

A long pause.

"Red," Sam said flatly. "His eyes are red."

Raincloud gave Dr. West a look, silent but clear. She grabbed her notepad and began to jot everything down in sharp, shorthand scribbles.

"Rebekka," Raincloud continued, "I want you to walk out of your bedroom now. Move through the house. Look carefully. Inside and outside. Tell me if you see anything... strange. Anything out of place. You'll know it when you see it."

He resumed his quiet prayer, a hum of syllables just above a whisper.

In her trance, Sam moved. She passed through the hallway, past the bedrooms, through the dining room, and into the kitchen.

The house was eerily quiet. Empty.

She stopped at the window.

And then she let out a long, aching gasp, followed by a guttural wail that cracked through the stillness of the room like glass shattering.

Raincloud closed his eyes. "I should have told her before she left the bedroom," he muttered to Dr. West. "This is what I feared."

Sam's cries tapered into sniffles.

"Rebekka," Raincloud said softly, still rubbing her hand. "Can you hear me?"

"Yes," she whispered.

"Good. I want you to calmly tell me what you see outside that window. Remember, you are only observing. You *feel* nothing. Do you understand?"

"Yes," she answered, voice steady but lifeless.

"There is a woman," she said. "She's naked... her skin is shredded. Hanging from a tree branch in the backyard."

Raincloud said nothing, waiting.

"There's also a boy," she continued. "A young boy. In a pot. Boiling over an open fire. He's naked too. Shredded."

Her tone was hollow. Flat. No emotion. Just words now.

"Rebekka," Raincloud said gently, "move away from the window. Close your eyes. Breathe."

He waited, then leaned in slightly. "You will remember only what you've told me here today, but only when I speak the name *Red Bear*. Do you understand?"

"Yes," Sam whispered.

"Good, Rebekka. Sleep now. Rest until I call you back."

He slowly released her hand, then loosened his grip on the pouch.

Sam's head lolled slightly to the side. Her body relaxed into the chair, as if she had simply fallen asleep.

Raincloud took in a deep breath and let it out slowly, then shook his head as if trying to clear the weight of what he'd just witnessed. "It's exactly what I feared... from the beginning, when you first told me about this case."

He leaned forward, rubbing his forehead before pulling a small towel from his pocket and wiping away the sheen of sweat that had gathered. His voice was calm, but heavy.

"The spirit has her father," he said at last. "That's why it has such power over her. That's why it knows how to control her. He's crossed over. The ritual she saw him perform, it wasn't just a ceremony. It was the crossing. The transformation."

He looked Dr. West in the eyes. "He became a skinwalker."

Dr. West's mouth fell slightly open, but she didn't speak.

"What Sam saw out the window," Raincloud continued, "that was her mother. And her younger brother. He killed them as part of the ritual. That was the price."

Dr. West's hand went to her chest, involuntarily. Her stomach twisted. "And… and Sam?"

"He didn't kill her," Raincloud said. "Because part of his spirit, his skinwalker essence, is bound inside her. If she dies before he figures out how to take it back, he dies too."

He leaned back slightly in his chair, the tension easing just a bit from his shoulders as he exhaled.

Dr. West's voice was quieter now. "What about the hibernation? How… how did she manage to lock it away for all those years?"

Raincloud paused, considering. "I can't fully figure that part out yet," he admitted. "But here's what I know."

He glanced toward the still-sleeping Sam, then back to Dr. West.

"It was a traumatic event, far beyond what a child should ever endure. But children… they carry great spiritual energy when they're young. Pure. Unfiltered. And in rare cases, powerful enough to protect themselves in ways even they don't understand."

He tapped his chest lightly. "She sealed it. Buried it deep. Everything connected to her father, his memory, his voice, his presence, was locked away, inaccessible even to her own conscious mind. That's why it vanished."

Dr. West's eyes filled with realization. "And it was unlocked... by another trauma."

Raincloud nodded.

Dr. West looked away, her voice dropping to nearly a whisper. "The doctors at the hospital said they don't understand how she survived the attempt. By all medical accounts, she should have died. But she didn't."

Raincloud's voice was soft now, edged with reverence. "Because the spirit tied her to this world. That moment, when she nearly crossed over, that's what pulled it out of hiding. That's what woke it up. That's why it's here again. And why it's not letting go."

"Rebekka, it's time to wake up."

Raincloud's voice was firm and commanding. Sam's eyes fluttered, then slowly opened.

"Wow," she muttered, rubbing her temples. "I sure hope you two found something this time, 'cause I feel like I've been hit by a semi."

She blinked a few times, her gaze drifting between Raincloud and Dr. West. Their expressions told her more than words could.

"Judging by those faces, I'm guessing this wasn't exactly good news... or maybe it was a good session with bad news attached?"

"Welcome back, Sam," Dr. West said gently. "Dr. Raincloud has uncovered quite a bit. Some of it... helpful. Some of it, hard to hear."

"Really?" Sam asked, leaning forward slightly, a spark of hope in her voice. "Is it gone? Am I finally free of it?"

Dr. West didn't answer right away. Her expression said everything before she opened her mouth.

"I'm sorry, Sam," she said. "There's still work to be done. But Dr. Raincloud may have a path forward."

Sam glanced over to the angel fountain outside the window, then turned her eyes back to

Raincloud. "Okay, Mr. Ra, Raincloud," she corrected herself, "what's the plan?"

Raincloud sat forward in his chair, his gaze steady and unreadable.

"Rebekka, this spirit won't leave on its own. It must be removed, most likely by force," he said. "Dr. West and I discussed this while you were under. And for now, we've agreed not to reveal the full truth about who or what this spirit really is. But I can tell you this: it is a *skinwalker*."

Sam stiffened, her eyes narrowing.

"This spirit is deceptive," Raincloud continued. "It can shift forms, usually into animals, but sometimes into more sinister shapes. It may appear in dreams, visions, or voices. It may claim to be a protector. A greater spirit. Even a god. Don't believe it. Ever. No matter what it promises. If you ever give yourself to it, willingly or not, if you *surrender*, you sign your own death certificate."

He let the words settle before adding, "It doesn't want you, Rebekka. It wants something *from* you. Something that allows it to keep surviving."

Sam glanced at Dr. West, then back to Raincloud. Her jaw tensed, her voice low and firm.

"Don't worry, Raincloud. I'm not giving in. That's the last thing I'd ever do."

Her look hardened. "That thing gets nothing from me, except an eviction notice."

A faint smile touched Raincloud's lips. He nodded with approval.

"So," Sam asked, voice still strong, "what's next? What do we do now?"

Raincloud exchanged a glance with Dr. West, then turned back to Sam.

"Rebekka," he said, "when's the last time you visited Cedar Lake, Connecticut?"

Chapter 11 - Comparing Notes

Fresno PD HQ

"Here are those enlarged photos you asked for. Sorry, it took longer than expected."

Ron handed the envelope over to Detective Rogers.

Rogers nodded, distracted. "Thanks, Ron. I wasn't gonna get to 'em until today anyway."

He slid the photos out of the envelope and spread them across his desk. Reaching into the side drawer, he pulled out his magnifying glass and hovered it over one of the images.

"Huh... what kind of feather is that?" he muttered. "Not sure I've ever seen anything quite like it."

Ron, still lingering in the doorway, heard him. "Oh, that?"

Rogers looked up. "Yeah. You got something to add about it? You didn't put anything in the shot, did you?"

Ron frowned. "No way. Why would I do that? That feather... it's not normal, Detective. It's mythological. Doesn't exist. At least, not in real life."

Rogers' brow furrowed. "Then what am I looking at?"

Ron stepped in, lowered his voice slightly. "They say it belongs to the Thunderbird. Native folklore. A creature of storms. Supposedly massive, with wings that create thunderclaps when it flies."

Rogers scoffed lightly. "So I've got a feather in a crime scene photo… from a bird that doesn't exist?"

Ron nodded. "I didn't see it when I took the pictures. It just showed up in that one frame. I can't explain it. It's above my pay grade, Detective."

Rogers leaned back in his chair, rubbing his temple. "Great. Add that to the pile of weird already circling this case."

He glanced at Ron again, brow still knit. "You sure you didn't doctor the image?"

"I'm sure. You want to send it out for verification, be my guest." Ron turned to go. "You done with me?"

"Yeah," Rogers muttered. "Yeah, you can go."

Ron disappeared down the hall, his footsteps fading.

Rogers looked back down at the photo, the strange feather captured in sharp clarity.

"A Thunderbird feather," he murmured to himself. "From a bird that lives in mythology. Wonderful."

Rogers sat back in his chair, staring at the monitor as the national database chugged away, sorting through keywords: *flayed skin, ritualistic killing, blood drained, large feather, Thunderbird.*

It was a long shot, and he knew it. His current cases, a pair of gruesome, unexplainable murders, were probably isolated. Some deranged lunatic high on bath salts, maybe something even darker. Still, the image Ron brought earlier, the feather that shouldn't exist, nagged at him like a splinter under the skin.

By late afternoon, the search finally pinged back with twelve hits.

Most were partials. A few had mentions of flayed skin. Some hinted at ritualistic elements, pentagrams, candles, or cryptic notes, but nothing cohesive. Only one stood out.

Location: *Chester, Connecticut – Cedar Lake Area*
Date: *Nearly twenty years ago*
Status: *Cold case*

Rogers muttered to himself, "Twenty years is a long time... what are the odds?"

Still, the similarities were there. Two initial victims, blood drained, bodies skin flayed, shredded, with deep incisions to the throat. One victim was found in a tree, and one in a pot of water. Oddest of all: mention of *a feather* found near both bodies, with no forensic relevance assigned. No photos, no lab analysis, no follow-up, just... dismissed.

Rogers leaned in. "Cedar Lake Serial Slasher," the file said. A string of killings that followed the same gruesome patterns, victims found dead, bloodless, sometimes with animal mutilations nearby. Local PD speculated on cult activity, but the case dried up when the murders abruptly stopped earlier this year.

There was a survivor listed for the original double homicide, but the name was redacted. Witness protection, maybe. Or local hush. The notes implied the town didn't want to talk. Not about the killer, and definitely not about the survivor.

Rogers exhaled and flipped to the last page of the old report. A name stood out: **Detective Mike Kirby**, lead on the original case.

"Guess I have to start somewhere," Rogers said, pulling his phone from his desk. "Might as well be with this guy... if he's still breathing."

"Uh, yeah, this is Detective Buk Rogers, yeah, yeah, spelled differently. I know, it's funny," he said, already tired of the usual reaction. "Anyway, I'm a detective with the Fresno, California PD, trying to reach Detective Mike Kirby. K-I-R-B-Y, Kirby. He was the lead on a double homicide about twenty years ago."

He leaned back as the hold music clicked on, some dusty jazz track that sounded like it was pulled from a gramophone. Rogers cringed.

"Man... this stuff could put a tweaker to sleep."

The line clicked again. "Detective Rogers? You still there?" came the voice of the Chester PD operator, a thick, nasally Northerner accent that made Rogers instinctively flinch.

"Still here. Great hold music, by the way," he said, full of sarcasm.

"Thanks... I guess. Detective Mike Kirby retired about ten years ago. He's no longer with the department here in Chester. Is there anything another detective might help you with?"

"Maybe, but would you happen to have Kirby's number? If he's still kickin', that is."

"Hang on. I'll check."

Cue the music again. Rogers closed his eyes and groaned. "Who even owns this music? Is this a cassette?"

Finally, the line clicked back. "Detective Rogers? Good news. Mike Kirby's still alive. One of our officers used to work with him, says he's not in good health, but still sharp as a tack. Talks with him pretty regularly."

"Well, that's good to hear. I mean the part about him being sharp, not the bad health."

There was a pause. "Right. Anyway, here's his number…"

The Chester PD operator rattled off the digits. Rogers jotted them down quickly.

"Anything else I can assist you with, Detective?"

"No, ma'am. That's all I need. Appreciate it."

"You're welcome. Have a nice day."

The line went dead. Rogers stared at the number scribbled on his notepad, chewing on the inside of his cheek.

"Great," he muttered. "Another damn phone call."

***

Phone Call – Detective Rogers to Mike Kirby

"Hello? Who is this? You selling something? How'd you get my number? If someone at the PD gave you my number, I'm gonna … "

"Detective Mike Kirby? Is this retired Detective Mike Kirby?"

"Uh... yeah. Who wants to know?"

Rogers already felt the call dragging and he hadn't even reached the meat of it. "Detective

Kirby, I'm Detective Rogers with the Fresno, California Police Department. I got your number from the Chester PD operator. I'm calling to ask about an old case you led about twenty years ago."

He intentionally left out his first name to dodge the jokes and puns he'd heard his whole life.

"Twenty years ago?" Kirby repeated. "That's a long time, Detective Rogers. What'd you say your first name was?"

Rogers sighed and braced for the punchline. "Buk."

"...Ah. Okay." No laughter. Just a pause. "Which case was it, Detective?"

Surprised at the lack of commentary, Rogers almost forgot why he called. "A case from the Cedar Lake area. Double homicide. Female victim, mid-thirties maybe, and a young boy, around four or five."

"Hmm... let me think," Kirby said, and Rogers could hear paper rustling on the other end, old case files, no doubt. A part of Rogers respected the man more for keeping his notes. He did the same.

"Here it is," Kirby said after a moment. "Yeah. That was a strange one. Can't believe this case is still open twenty years later. That part of town, down by the lake... strange place. And the people? Just as strange."

"Strange how?" Rogers leaned forward, now more invested. Kirby sounded like he knew the lay of the land.

"They didn't care much for the police, that side of the lake. Kind of like a commune. All the same type of people. Mostly Native Americans, Indians. Don't bother asking what tribe; no one could ever say. I think it was a mix. Most of them were loggers. Kept to themselves. Only came into Chester for supplies. Didn't even have a school over there, so the kids got bused into town."

"A closed community, then."

"Yeah. Closed tight." Kirby exhaled hard. "So, the double homicide... woman was flayed, skinned like a deer. Torn to pieces. Poor thing. Looked like a cult killing, but there were details that didn't fit the usual ritual murders. And the boy..."

Kirby paused. His voice cracked ever so slightly. "It still turns my guts when I think about the boy. Same deal, shredded. But he wasn't hung up like his mother. No... he was in a pot. Partially consumed. Damnedest thing I've ever seen. Damnedest thing any of us ever saw."

Rogers swallowed, pen frozen above his notepad.

"There were two feathers found," Kirby continued. "One by each victim. We couldn't identify the bird. Looked diseased, maybe. Eventually dismissed them as a coincidence, probably some dead bird nearby. We never photographed them. No real records, just mentioned in the file."

"What about the father?" Rogers asked.

"Never found him. Husband, father, gone. We searched part of the lake, figured animals got him. Saw tracks all around that area. Couldn't rule anything out, him or someone else."

"And the survivor?"

"Yeah. A girl. Sam, or Rebecca, Rebecca Logan, if I remember right. Poor thing didn't remember a damn thing. Not about the murder, not about the days before it. Blank slate. I was afraid she was somehow involved, or maybe just saw too much and shut down. Honestly thought she'd end up in a state facility somewhere, but they sent her to a foster center instead."

Rogers jolted. The name hit something in his brain. Sam... Logan. Could it be?

"You said her name was Rebecca Logan?"

"That's what I have here in my notes. Sam or Rebecca Logan."

Rogers was scribbling like mad. The name rang a bell, loudly, but he couldn't place where he'd heard it recently.

"What about the other murders in the area? The serial ones?"

Kirby shifted. "Yeah, those. After the double homicide, we had a string of killings around the lake. All strange. Looked somewhat ritualistic, people had their throats cut, blood drained, and animals mutilated. We figured some cult had moved in and was hiding deep in the woods. Never caught them, though. Most victims were homeless, drifters,

269

people no one missed. Never could tie it all together. And with the lack of cooperation from the lakeside folks, we couldn't get far. The serial murders ended here recently, but I don't have much else on them. I haven't really stayed on top of those since I retired. That's been about ten years.

He rustled more paper. "Honestly, I think we redacted the animal deaths. There was just too much weird in that one area."

Rogers leaned back in his chair, mind racing. A survivor named Samantha Logan. A flayed mother. A half-eaten boy in a boiling pot. A feather no one could explain, like the one in his photos.

Something was connecting. Something big.

"Detective Kirby," Rogers said slowly, "you've been a massive help."

"I've got one last question for you before I let you go," Rogers said, leaning forward in his chair. "You sound like you kept pretty meticulous notes on your investigation. Do you think that, if I brought out my case files, we could sit down together and compare? Maybe find all the similarities? That is, if my captain approves, and if you're willing to look at mine while I go through yours."

"Mmm," Kirby said, voice thoughtful. "I don't have anything else going on around here. Sifting through some case info would feel like old times. Sure, I'd be willing, Detective Rogers. But you're quite a ways away, being out there in California. You make it here, and we'll go through it."

Rogers exhaled. He needed to get out, clear his head, and Kirby sounded like a version of himself ten or twenty years further down the line. "I'll run it by my superiors. I doubt they'll have any issues, especially if there's a chance these cases are connected. I'll give you a call back with travel details. You'll hear from me later today or tomorrow at the latest. I really appreciate your help, Detective Kirby."

"Sounds like a plan, Detective Rogers. See ya now."

Click.

Kirby hung up.

Detective Rogers closed the case file on his desk and walked straight into his captain's office. He laid

271

out the case details and his suspicions about the possible links between the recent Fresno murders and the cold cases from Chester. The captain agreed, too many parallels to ignore. The trip was greenlit.

Rogers found a flight into New Haven, Connecticut. Chester's airport was too small for commercial flights, so he'd have to drive the final leg.

Later that afternoon, Rogers picked up the phone and called Detective Kirby back.

"Got my travel set," he said. "I'll be flying into New Haven, then driving out your way. Should be in Chester by tomorrow evening."

***

Back at the Dragon Tattoo and Piercing Shop
The back door to the shop opened, and in walked Sam, no worse for wear and, surprisingly, in good spirits.

"Sam! I'm so glad to see you back here. I've missed you, and you're missing the rush in clients we've been getting." Julie rushed over to greet her.

Sam smiled, genuinely glad to be back, even if it was just for a few short hours.

"Jules, I'm glad to see you, too. I've got more info to share with you, stuff I didn't have time to explain over the phone earlier. Let me just get back in the swing, help these new clients, and we'll catch up later in the back."

Julie's smile never faded, but she could already sense Sam had something deeper to say, maybe something she wouldn't like.

Being back in the shop felt almost normal again. Sam let the morning's session with Dr. West and Raincloud fade into the background. She'd have time to think about that tomorrow, when she and Raincloud flew out to Chester, Connecticut.

She and Julie chatted off and on throughout the rush and during quiet moments between clients. It felt good, better than good. Sam couldn't remember the last time she felt this grounded... or the last time they'd been this busy.

As the evening wore on and the sun began to set, foot traffic outside the shop thinned. Julie looked over at Sam, who was cleaning her station and dancing a little to the beat of the music playing overhead.

"Hey," Julie called over, "you wanna take a break? We can head out back and sit, you can fill me in on what happened this morning."

"Yep," Sam replied. "Just let me finish wiping down my machine. I'll meet you out back at the table."

Julie headed to the back, grabbed two lemon teas from the fridge, and sat down to wait. A minute later, Sam slipped through the curtain, walked over, and dropped into the seat across from her.

"Man, this place has been *rockin'* today. Was it this busy the other day I missed? If we keep this up, we're gonna treat ourselves to a trip to some small island in the Caribbean and finally relax." Sam wiped pretend sweat from her forehead and gave Julie a wrinkled-nose grin.

"Okay, Sam," Julie said, leaning in with her elbows on the table, hands under her chin, "spill it. I want to know as much as you feel comfortable telling me."

"Well," Sam began, cracking open her tea, "I told you most everything this morning, why I was heading to Dr. West's office yesterday and again today. Based on what I found out this morning... well, I have to fly to Chester, Connecticut tomorrow."

Julie raised an eyebrow but said nothing.

"It's a long story," Sam continued, "one I *promise* to tell you when I get back. But I *can* tell you this, it has to do with my family's disappearance. I might finally find out what happened to them. This could give me the chance to close that chapter of my life. And then maybe, *finally*, I can focus fully on the here and now. On our shop. On my future."

She paused and smiled softly. "Julie... I feel like I can see the light at the end of the tunnel. I don't know if I'm ready for what I might find, but at least I'll have answers. Maybe even closure."

Julie sat quietly, listening intently. She had questions, *a lot* of questions, but she wasn't going to dig. Not yet. If Sam had a shot at closure, Julie wanted that for her more than anything.

She wanted her friend back, the cocky, determined, independent Sam she'd met at that tattoo convention. And if this trip to Connecticut could bring that version of her back? Then Julie would support her all the way.

Chapter 12 - Chester and Cedar Lake

In flight next day

Looking out the airplane window, watching clouds drift by and the tiny green and brown squares of the country blur beneath them, Sam sat in deep thought.

Should she have told Julie more? She probably deserved to know. Julie had been Sam's rock, ever since their friendship had deepened into something solid, something real. Sam decided, when... *if*... she got through this, she would tell Julie everything. No more half-truths. No more hiding.

Her thoughts drifted to the return ahead, to her hometown, to Cedar Lake, where everything had started... and ended. One moment, she was a happy little girl, and the next? An outcast. Torn from everything she knew. Forced to live a whole other life as if the first one had never existed. She still didn't understand why her relatives had cast her out so easily. They had once loved her, or at least it felt like love. They gave her handmade trinkets, blankets, and carved dolls. She would've never guessed that the same people would one day

277

abandon her, turning their backs on their own flesh and blood.

Her mind shifted to the man seated beside her, Raincloud.

She didn't know much about him. They had only just met yesterday in Dr. West's office. But even in that short time, he had become something… a presence. Someone willing to drop everything to help her. Someone who didn't just *believe* her, but understood what she was facing, and who was flying across the country to face it with her. That meant something.

She still felt nervous. But also… determined. Whatever was waiting in Cedar Lake, she was going to face it.

Raincloud was old, yes, but wise, steady. There was a comfort in him she hadn't expected. Almost like the comfort she remembered from her father… before everything changed. If only Dr. West could have come too. But Raincloud said it was better that she didn't. Sam still didn't understand why, but Dr. West did. Even if it pained her. Even if it felt like she was sending her own daughter off into danger.

There were things, Sam knew it, things Raincloud and Dr. West hadn't told her. For her own protection, maybe. And even though that stung, she understood it wasn't meant out of spite.

Surprisingly, she had slept well the night before. After closing the shop, Julie insisted Sam spend the night at her place. Julie and Ron had driven her over to her apartment so she could pack. They waited while she gathered what she needed for the trip, then brought her back with them.

They talked about everything *except* the trip. Played some old records. Had a couple of drinks. Laughed more than Sam expected. It was the most peace she'd felt in weeks.

In the morning, Julie and Ron drove her to the Fresno airport. Julie hugged her hard before letting go, whispering that she hoped Sam found the closure she needed and came back safe.

Sam met Raincloud at the gate. Somehow, as always, he was already there, quiet, waiting. Like a ghost. He always seemed to arrive before she did… and disappear before she had time to say goodbye.

Now, high above the country, she looked over at him again. Raincloud sat silently, eyes closed, hands resting lightly on his lap.

She couldn't tell if he was sleeping… or meditating.

Sam's mind shifted again, to the voice. The dark shadow of smoke from her visions.

It hadn't made a sound since the encounter with Raincloud.

She had fully expected it to torment her all night, whispering from the edges of sleep, pushing into her dreams to punish her for what Raincloud had dredged up. That was its style, lurking in the corners, waiting for the moment she felt safest to strike.

But… nothing.

Not even a whisper.

No dreams. No visions. Just silence.

And for once, Sam was perfectly fine with that. She'd take silence over twisted dreams and guttural voices any day.

Still, the quiet unnerved her just a little. It felt… calculated.

As if the spirit was watching. Waiting. Planning something.

Maybe Raincloud had scared it off.

Or maybe it was hiding deeper, burrowing down, regaining strength.

Sam exhaled softly and looked back out the window, deciding not to chase the thought further. Not here. Not now. There would be time for darkness later, if it showed up again.

Right now, she had a plane to land, a town to return to, and truths to uncover.

The plane landed and taxied to the gate. Sam and Raincloud moved through the terminal without much conversation, retrieved their luggage, and headed out to the rental lot. They chose a silver Rogue, simple, anonymous, and tossed their bags into the back. Neither of them had packed much.

Sam hadn't planned to stay long. Just long enough to do what needed to be done, get the answers, and go back home.

Raincloud offered to drive, saying he enjoyed seeing the countryside roll past, that the Great Spirit had His handiwork stretched out across this land like brushstrokes on canvas. Sam figured it was more than just a love for scenery. Raincloud didn't speak much during the drive, and when he did, his voice carried the weight of focus. She guessed he was already searching inward, listening, preparing himself for whatever waited for them out at Cedar Lake.

He did mention they would need to stop at the police station first. Let them know they were in town and headed to the old home site. Not out of courtesy, but out of necessity. Raincloud didn't expect much help from law enforcement. He said the real resistance would come from the community itself, the people who still lived near Cedar Lake. The ones Sam once called neighbors.

"They will not be welcoming," he had said flatly. "Some places hold onto secrets like they're sacred. Even when those secrets rot everything around them."

After twenty years, the old home might not even be standing. If the land had been left to reclaim it, there might be nothing left but timbers and bones.

The drive from New Haven to Chester was just under an hour, winding east through thick woods and scattered farmland. Sam watched the landscape go by, looking for anything familiar, anything to jolt a memory. But it was all foggy, blank. Like someone had whitewashed over her childhood.

She turned to Raincloud, who looked deep in thought, hands steady on the wheel, gaze forward.

"What do you expect to find at Cedar Lake, Raincloud?" she asked. "Is the spirit there? A ghost? What should I prepare for?"

He was silent for several moments, the hum of the tires on asphalt the only reply. She could see him working through the question, measuring his answer carefully. Not out of secrecy, but caution. She could feel it. He wasn't hiding from her. He was hiding from the thing that might be listening.

Finally, he spoke. His tone was low, measured.

"Rebekka, I cannot say for certain what we'll find tonight. I've been meditating, on the plane, now in the car, seeking guidance from my spirit guides. They're quiet... but not absent. They're waiting. Watching. They'll speak when the time is right."

He turned his head slightly toward her, then back to the road.

"For now, enjoy the peace. Look out at this land, it holds truth, even if memory has buried it. The past is coming, child. But let it come on its own. We don't need to chase it yet."

***

Chester, Connecticut – Arrival of Detective Buk Rogers

Detective Rogers grabbed his small bag from the baggage carousel, scanned the overhead signs, and tried to make sense of the maze that was New Haven Airport. He'd traveled before, but it had been a while. Airports were louder now, more chaotic, or maybe he was just older and crankier. Probably both.

After a few detours and too many wrong turns, he finally found the rental car lot. He didn't have many choices, so he picked the Nissan Rogue. Silver, blah, but better than cramming himself into a

Chevy Trax like a circus bear. He tossed his bag
into the back seat, punched the address into the
NAV system, and pulled out toward the highway.

The drive to Chester was just over an hour. Not
much traffic, no sirens, no shouting on the streets.
Just trees, winding roads, and the low hum of tires
on asphalt. Peaceful. Different than Fresno.

He found it gave him time to think.

The case had been looping in his head since he
left California. Two victims, shredded, blood
drained, mysterious feather left behind. And now a
twenty-year-old case in Connecticut with matching
details. Maybe it was a long shot, but something
about the old crime scene, and the fact that those
murders just stopped, didn't sit right. Then there
were the victims: in both towns, mostly vagrants,
forgotten people on the edges. Easy targets. He
didn't think it was a coincidence.

"Chester Welcomes You," the sign said as he
crossed into town.

The NAV chirped and guided him to the small
police department. Rogers pulled into the lot,
stepped out, and stretched, arms overhead, spine

285

popping from the flight and the long drive. He made his way inside.

The front lobby was quiet, small-town simple. He approached the courtesy desk.

"Excuse me, can you direct me to the duty officer?" he asked.

The woman behind the desk looked up, her face neutral.

"May I ask your name and reason for the visit, sir?"

"Yes, ma'am. Detective Rogers, Fresno PD. I'm in town to review a homicide that happened about twenty years ago. I believe it may be linked to two open cases back in Fresno. Just wanted to let the DO know I'm here, in case anything comes up."

She blinked slowly. "Detective Rogers, alright. I'll take your name, department, and badge number and pass them along to the duty officer when he returns. He's out to lunch right now."

Rogers nodded, scribbled the info she requested, and handed it over.

"Thanks," he said. He started toward the door, then stopped, turned back.

"Actually… any chance you could recommend a good spot for a late lunch?"

The woman didn't look up. "Diner down the street, two blocks. On the right. You'll probably see a couple patrol cars out front, our folks like the place."

"Much appreciated," he said, tipping an invisible hat as he walked out.

Sure enough, two blocks later, he found a tiny diner with two marked units parked out front.

"This must be it," he muttered. He pulled in, parked, and headed inside.

***

Raincloud and Sam Arrive in Chester

The sign ahead read "Chester Welcomes You." Raincloud saw it before Sam. He nodded toward it. "Rebekka, would you like to stop for a bite? Could be a long night, and having something in our stomachs might help us think more clearly. Those plane snacks shouldn't legally be called food. The coffee... eh, it was tolerable."

He gave a slight grin, one of the few she'd seen from him.

Sam glanced over, catching the faint spark of humor. "I could eat. My nerves are still on edge, but I think I can keep something down."

They pulled into a small diner just off the main road. It was squat and unassuming, with a faded Coca-Cola sign in the window and two marked patrol cars parked out front.

"Might be a good sign if the local law eats here," Raincloud said, pointing toward the units.

They parked and stepped inside, the bell over the door chiming gently. It smelled of coffee, grease, and something baking, possibly pie. They found a booth in the back, away from the windows and most of the other diners.

Sam sank into the vinyl seat, feeling the weight of the day start to settle in her bones. Flying cross-country was always exhausting, and the added drive from New Haven hadn't helped. She might not sleep much on a normal night, but this morning had started early, and it wasn't close to ending.

She scanned the laminated menu without really reading it. "Chicken salad," she told the waitress. "Water, and lemon wedges, please."

Raincloud ordered a club sandwich and a glass of unsweetened tea.

They ate slowly, not talking much. The silence wasn't heavy, just thoughtful, each of them turning inward, mentally preparing for what lay ahead. The taste of food was grounding, but Sam's thoughts were far from this place. Her eyes drifted to the window now and then, catching glimpses of the small-town street beyond. It felt familiar and foreign at the same time.

She didn't know what was waiting for them at Cedar Lake.

But she could feel it pulling her back.

***

Detective Rogers in the Diner

Detective Rogers sat at a small table near the back of the diner, a manila folder spread open before him. Inside were case notes, photographs, scribbled observations, and the address for retired Detective Mike Kirby.

The waitress came by and took his order, something simple, nothing fried. She barely broke stride as she jotted it down and turned away.

Rogers flipped through the notes on his two open cases, then pulled out the details he'd jotted down during his call with Kirby. He began cross-referencing, looking for anything, even a sliver, that could link the mutilations in Fresno to the cold case in Cedar Lake.

He ate slowly, barely tasting the food as he sifted through ink and memory. He'd been at this long enough to know when something *felt* right, and these cases... something about them was aligned.

When he was done, he slid the notes back into the folder, tucked it under his arm, and paid the tab at the register. As he turned toward the door, his eyes swept the diner, instinct more than curiosity.

In a booth near the back, he noticed an older man with a calm, quiet presence. Something about him snagged Rogers' attention. He looked Native, maybe Lakota or Navajo, and for a moment, Rogers felt a flicker of recognition.

He resembled someone Rogers had met years ago, when he was a new detective stationed in Oregon, still green, still idealistic. That man had been a medicine man, consulted unofficially by a few rural departments in cold or strange cases.

Rogers slowed. Thought about approaching the man. But then shook it off.

What would a medicine man from Oregon be doing here in a sleepy Connecticut town like Chester? That wasn't likely. Just a coincidence, he told himself.

Rogers pushed through the glass door and stepped into the warm, late-afternoon air. He glanced across the parking lot and saw another rental car that looked identical to the one he was driving. What are the chances of running into another out-of-towner with the same taste in cars all the way out here in Chester? Rogers laughed to himself. He located his own rental and slid behind the wheel, started the engine, and headed toward Kirby's place just a few miles down the road.

Detective Buk Rogers - Newly promoted to Detective in Oregon

Almost fifteen years before transferring to the Fresno PD as a senior detective, Buk Rogers was a newly promoted investigator with the Springfield Police Department in Oregon. His first solo assignment came quickly, a homicide just outside the Grande Ronde reservation.

Although Rogers had previously assisted more seasoned detectives, this was his first time leading a case. It came with extra scrutiny; the victim was tied to the reservation, and jurisdictional tensions were always a factor. To help navigate the cultural and procedural boundaries, Rogers was given the name of a local tribesman: Raincloud.

Raincloud was respected by both local and tribal police. He had a reputation for finding people, sometimes fugitives, sometimes the missing, and doing so with near-perfect success. No one in the Springfield department could (or would) explain exactly how he achieved his results, but his recovery rate hovered at an uncanny ninety-nine percent.

With Raincloud's help, Rogers solved the homicide while keeping the fragile peace between the communities. It was the start of a professional respect, and friendship, that lasted through Rogers's years in Springfield. But after his move to Fresno, their contact faded… until fate brought them together again.

***

Sam and Raincloud Leave the Diner

Sam and Raincloud finished their lunch in silence; each lost in thought about what lay ahead. Raincloud rose from the booth and walked up to the register to pay the bill, while Sam stepped outside into the fading daylight. She pulled out her phone and called Julie to let her know they'd arrived in Chester and were making a quick stop at the police department before heading to her old homestead.

"Not sure what we'll find," she told her friend, "but hopefully it'll bring some kind of closure."

Raincloud met her by the car just as she ended the call. He glanced up the street, toward the building they'd passed earlier. "That's the local PD," he said. "Covers both Cedar Lake and the township. We'll check in, let them know we're here, and then head out."

They drove the short distance and parked in front of the squat brick building. Raincloud went inside alone. Sam stayed in the car, her gaze drifting across the sleepy townscape, her mind drifting further still.

She tried to recall anything about this place. A flash of memory surfaced, she was much younger, sitting in a sterile room under harsh lights, a detective gently asking her questions. But she couldn't remember what they were or how she had answered. What she did recall was the white van that came afterward. *Heritage Home*, it said in blue, no, black, letters across the side. She couldn't remember where they took her, only that she never came back.

As she stared out the passenger window, a chill ran down her spine. That creeping, invisible sensation that she was being watched. Not from outside the car, not even from inside, but through her. Like something staring out from the place behind her eyes. The thought of the shadow man, the voice like smoke, sent a ripple of fear through her.

The driver's door opened suddenly, and she jumped.

"You're nervous, Rebekka." Raincloud settled into the seat, his voice low but attentive. "Are you feeling something? Remembering something? Is there anything I should know?"

Sam looked at him for a long second, then shook her head. She wasn't sure if it was nerves or something worse. No sense stirring things up until she knew for sure.

Raincloud gave a slow nod. "If anything changes, if something feels strange or wrong, or if the spirit speaks again, you must tell me. We need to keep this journey hidden from it, as long as we can."

He reached over and touched her hand. With his other hand, he gripped the small pouch that hung from a cord around his neck. He closed his eyes, murmuring something under his breath. Sam sat perfectly still, her hand beneath his, listening to the faint rustle of leaves outside the car.

When he opened his eyes again, his expression had changed, calm, but wary.

"The spirit moves," he said softly, "but it hasn't seen us yet."

He released her hand with a reassuring tap, then started the engine. A narrow road wound east through the woods. Raincloud followed the handwritten directions the officer at the station had given him, steering the car toward the place where Sam's past lay buried in the trees.

After a long moment, Raincloud broke the silence.

"Rebekka, before we arrive, I must tell you the truth, about the spirit… and who it once was."

Chapter 13 - Rebekka's Forgotten Memories

"Rebecca…Rebecca, where'd you get off to? I thought we were both scrubbing the floor?"

"Mommy, I didn't mean to. It was only a second, I promise."

Sam's mother came around the doorway into Jason's small bedroom. Sam was sitting in the corner, her arms wrapped tightly around Jason as if protecting him from something unseen.

"Sam, what on earth are you going on about? Why did you leave me to scrub the floor all alone?" Mary Logan stood in the doorway, one hand on her hip and the other still gripping the scrub brush.

"Rebecca, come on, let's get back to work. You can play with Jason later."

"I can't, Mommy. I, I looked after you told me not to. I didn't mean to, I promise."

Mary walked over to where Sam was still crouched in the corner and knelt beside her and Jason.

"Rebecca, what did you see? What was it? Did you see anything? You've got to tell me." Mary dropped the scrub brush, cupped Sam's cheeks in both hands, and looked directly into her eyes.

"Rebecca, what did you see?"

"I, I saw dancing black smoke with red eyes, Mommy. It looked directly at me, so I came back here to protect Jason."

"Oh my…"

At that, Mary stood up and ran out of the room, down the short hallway, and out the back door. Sam remained frozen in place, holding Jason close. From where she sat, she could hear yelling in the backyard, loud, frantic. She had never heard her mama raise her voice at anyone, but now she was screaming at Sam's dad.

Sam couldn't make out the words. The back door suddenly slammed open, and heavy footsteps came down the hall. Her daddy's breathing was loud, ragged. He stormed down the hallway, shirtless, hair soaked and wild, sweat dripping down his flushed face.

"REBECCA! REBECCA, where are you, girl?"

He appeared in the doorway like a thundercloud. Sam looked up, eyes wide and trembling.

"What did you see, Rebecca? What was it?"

She began to cry, not understanding why what she'd seen was so bad. In between sobs, she told him everything, how the black smoke had danced in the fire, how it had red eyes, and how it looked straight at her.

Her daddy dropped to his knees, buried his face in his sweating hands, and let out a muffled scream.

Then, without a word, he stood up and walked away, back out the back door.

A few moments later, Mary returned. She stepped silently into Jason's room, gently lifted him from Sam's lap, and said softly, "Go to your room, Rebecca. Sit there. Alone. Mommy and Daddy need to talk."

From that point on, Sam spent most of her days locked away in her room.

Soon after, she began talking to someone, someone her mother never saw. Mary would sometimes stand outside the door and listen. Sam's voice was clear, animated, sometimes whispering, sometimes giggling softly, but there was always a pause, as if someone was answering back.

Her father, Harry, never entered Sam's room directly. But late at night, after Mary and Jason had gone to bed, he would sit outside her door or just inside the frame, and the two of them would talk in hushed tones, too quiet to make out. Mary asked Sam once what they talked about.

"It's a secret, Mama," Sam had said, eyes wide and sincere. "One day, you and Jason will be part of it too. But not yet."

Mary didn't like secrets in her house, especially not ones between her daughter and husband, but she let it go, brushing it off as a child's imagination. Mostly.

Harry began disappearing for days at a time after that. He would run off into the woods past the lake without saying a word. While he was gone, the voices in Sam's room grew louder and more frequent. Mary would sometimes hear her daughter speaking and laughing with someone, or something, through the door. When she opened it, she always found Sam alone. Sometimes asleep in bed. Other times, sitting cross-legged on the floor, eyes closed or staring off at nothing.

Mary tried not to pry. She told herself it was just a phase, or that Harry would fix it when he got back.

But Harry came home a stranger each time. His clothes were often missing, torn, or soaked through with sweat, and what looked like blood. He always bathed in the shallow edge of the lake before stepping foot back into the house. Mary asked no questions. She didn't dare.

That was when Harry's family stopped coming over. The weekend cookouts came to a quiet, unspoken end. No more laughing kids in the yard. No more folding chairs around the pit fire.

Mary started having nightmares. Bad ones. Ones she couldn't shake. She began sleeping with Jason in her bed, holding him close as though she feared he might disappear.

The house grew still. Cold. The warmth that once filled its walls was gone.

It wasn't a home anymore.

There were no more birthday parties. No more school. Sam stopped attending altogether. She became reclusive, refusing to come out of her room. Mary had to go in daily just to clean up after her. Sam no longer used the bathroom. Instead, she urinated and defecated in the corners like a caged animal. Mary began bathing her with a bucket, because if she tried anything else, Sam would fight, screaming to be left alone.

Mary had never seen a child, let alone her own nine-year-old daughter, slip into something so feral.

That's when she decided she was leaving. She would take Jason and go, go west, back to her family, if they were even still alive. She hadn't seen or spoken to them since they moved to Connecticut, but it didn't matter. She had to get her son away from this madness. She couldn't take the mental and emotional abuse any longer, being left alone in a house where her daughter had become something unrecognizable.

Harry didn't argue. He simply told her that Sam had to stay locked away. "What she saw that day," he'd whispered, "it'll overtake her. It already is."

302

And he was right. Mary saw it happening more and more every day.

One week later, two days before she planned to leave, it happened.

She and Jason were out back. Mary had filled the old wash pot, the one they used for play and the occasional bath when the water heater went out. She was washing Jason, humming quietly, the evening sun casting long shadows through the trees.

That's when something came out of the woods.

Mary caught only a glimpse before it reached them. The face, it looked like Harry's. But the body was monstrous. Part man, part beast. Long limbs. Huge claws. Coarse, matted hair covered its arms and chest. And its eyes, its eyes glowed red like burning rubies.

The creature moved with terrifying speed.

One swipe of its massive arm broke Mary's delicate neck. She crumpled to the ground without a sound. Jason turned to look, confused, his little mouth forming a question that never made it out.

The second strike crushed his small skull like a tin can.

He never even saw the thing coming.

With both mother and son dead, the creature lifted Mary's limp body and hung her from a low cedar branch. With eerie precision, it peeled her skin away, the way a hunter skins a kill. It placed clay jars beneath her, collecting her blood in silence.

Then it turned to Jason.

It pulled his body from the pot, flayed him open, and drained what blood remained. Then, as if mocking the innocence of it all, the creature placed him back into the pot. A fire roared beneath it, and the water began to boil.

The transformation came after.

The beast's form began to shift, legs straightening, claws retracting into fingers and toes. Hair receded, crawling backward across the limbs like retreating shadows. The monstrous face folded in on itself, reshaping, softening... until only a man remained.

The hair on his head still wild. But the rest, human.

And familiar.

Then a noise came from within the house, quick footsteps running across wooden floors, followed by the slam of a door and loud, choking sobs echoing down through the walls.

The man, who had been the beast only moments before, stepped into the house, blood still dripping from his hands and lips. He paused in the entryway, listening. No one in sight, but the sobbing was unmistakable, trembling down the hallway like a pulse.

He moved slowly, deliberately. The hallway stretched before him, and the first door was shut. Behind it, the sobs were louder, gasping, ragged. The man placed his hand on the knob and turned it gently. The door creaked open.

There, crouched in the center of the room, was Sam. Her back was turned, and she was clutching one of Jason's toys, rocking slowly back and forth. She said nothing.

The man stepped into the corner of the room, his eyes fixed on the girl. Silent. Predatory.

He began to chant in a tongue long forgotten, an ancient language spoken only by Skinwalkers. Words not meant for the living.

He knew what had to happen.

She needed to die. The girl. Her blood would complete the ritual. It would finally grant him the full transformation. No more in-between. No more half-man, half-beast. He was ready.

But before he could act, Sam turned.

Her eyes were red, not from crying, but from something else entirely. Something inside.

And then a voice came from her lips.

But it wasn't her voice.

"Do not kill her," it said. Sleek and slippery, like smoke crawling across glass. "If you do, we both die."

The man froze.

"She must relinquish me first," the voice hissed. "We have to be one before you are complete. After that… she's yours."

Sam sat motionless, eyes wide, voice borrowed. The essence of the Skinwalker, the very thing her father had been trying to merge with, was inside her now, bound to her.

Trapped.

Within her mind, Sam stood in a darkened room, alone, confused. The presence coiled around her, suffocating, whispering, trying to take root.

But Sam, even at nine years old, was stronger than anyone imagined.

She took back her body.

Her eyes cleared, only for a moment, and she looked at the man. The thing. The beast who killed her mother. Her brother. The man who had once been her father.

And her mind shattered.

Not with screams. Not with words. It simply collapsed in on itself, unable to hold the weight of what she had seen. Unable to process the horror of it all. Like a mirror dropped from too high, it fractured, hiding away the pieces.

She folded everything into the deepest recesses of her mind. All the memories of that day. Of her father. Of the fire. The blood. The voice. All of it, locked behind walls no one could see. Not even her.

And in doing so, Sam did more than bury the trauma.

She imprisoned the essence.

The Skinwalker, half-bonded, incomplete, was trapped inside her. Sealed within a child's psyche. And her father, no longer fully man, not fully monster, was cursed to remain in between. Stuck.

Until the day he could reclaim the essence.

Until Sam remembered.

***

Rogers and Kirby

"I'd still swear it was a cult of some sort," Kirby muttered, shaking his head. "But with twenty years in between, and the same thing, almost to a T, it just can't be cult-like. Doesn't add up. Something here doesn't make sense. And then, lo and behold… the feather. The same damn feather."

He set the old crime scene photos beside the new ones, taken just two or three weeks ago, and leaned back in his chair. The lines on his face deepened as he rubbed his whiskery chin, then took another long sip of coffee.

"I don't know anymore," he said, voice low. "After seeing your two cases, Rogers, they look as if they happened the very next day after mine. Not two decades later."

Detective Rogers nodded, his brow tight in thought.

"I'm with you, Kirby. Cults don't take twenty-year sabbaticals, go completely underground, and then pop back up with exactly the same M.O. Doesn't happen. You and I both know that. Something else is going on here, something... outside the ordinary."

He paused, letting that sit a moment, then added, "And why is it that the weirdest things that land on my desk always seem to trace back to the Natives? I had a contact once, used to consult him on these kinds of matters. But that was a long time ago. He's probably still in Oregon."

Rogers brushed back his hair, then took a sip of Kirby's coffee.

"Damn good coffee, by the way. Beats the hell out of that Fresno stuff. Too weak. Too much fufu."

Kirby let out a dry chuckle. "You're welcome. No syrup or whipped cream here, just honest beans and hot water."

Rogers nodded, then motioned to the folder on the table.

"You mind if I take these with me tonight? Just want to study the terrain, compare locations, and cross-reference the details. Scouts honor. I'll bring them back exactly how I got them."

He raised three fingers in the Boy Scout salute.

Kirby smirked. "Sure. I trust you now. You're like a younger me, though not that much younger."

They shared a laugh, but Kirby's tone turned serious, flat.

"Let me be direct with you, Rogers. Don't trust the people in that commune. Don't turn your back on them. They've got their own ways, and they hide more than they share. I wouldn't be surprised if that old home place isn't standing anymore. The land around Cedar Lake… it has a way of taking back what was once its own. Houses. Cars. Animals."

He paused.

"People."

His voice was quiet, but heavy. A warning buried beneath the words.

Rogers gave a slow nod. "I'll keep that in mind. I appreciate the help, and the collaboration. I'll be back to return everything before I head back to Fresno. That work for you?"

"Sure. Tomorrow, or the day after."

Rogers extended a hand, tipping an imaginary hat before shaking Kirby's firmly.

"If we crack this wide open, I'll owe you a drink."

"You crack this case," Kirby said with a half-smile, "hell, I'll open the good whiskey."

They both laughed, a flicker of ease in the heaviness between them.

Rogers stepped out of Kirby's house, slid into the Rogue, and drove off, heading toward Cedar Lake.

Toward whatever was waiting for them all.

***

Raincloud and Sam

Sam looked at Raincloud, her face etched with concern for what he was about to tell her. She wasn't even sure she wanted to know who, or what, the spirit inside her really was.

Raincloud pulled the car into a rest stop overlooking the lake and the surrounding landscape. He shut off the engine.

"Let's get out," he said. "I'd rather we talk outside the car, where there's more space... and where we can see the land we're heading toward."

Sam stepped out, followed by Raincloud. They walked around the car to a covered lookout with a waist-high stone wall. The wind coming off the lake was cool, and the hush of the trees gave the place a solemn stillness.

"Rebekka," Raincloud said, "I've been turning this over in my mind since we first uncovered the truth in Dr. West's office. I know this isn't going to be easy to hear, but it's something you need to know before we continue on this path."

He paused, then looked her square in the eyes.

"The spirit, the shadow you and Dr. West described, is old. But it's not as old as it wants you to believe. It masquerades as an ancient force, something older than time itself. But that's a ruse. A lie."

Sam narrowed her eyes, listening carefully.

"The spirit inside you is what we call a skinwalker. Or, in some traditions, a shapeshifter. These spirits are old, yes, but not primeval. They mimic others. They impersonate people, animals... and in rare cases, other spirits. Their true intentions are often hidden. And the ways they come to inhabit people or creatures vary: sometimes by touch, sometimes through killing, and, most rarely, through direct eye contact."

Raincloud's expression grew more serious.

"When they want to possess someone or something... they usually kill the host first. That's what makes your case so rare, and, thankfully, so fortunate. It didn't take your life."

Sam nodded, her mind trying to grasp the weight of what he was saying. She could understand the words, but the meaning, the why, still escaped her.

313

"This spirit came to you through eye contact, back when you were just a child," Raincloud said. "From what I've learned, both from my own digging and Dr. West's research, your father, Harry Logan, was Native, like I am. Like you are. There's a ritual... an old one... that can turn a human into a skinwalker. It's not often performed, but some have attempted it, to live forever, to walk the earth feeding off others, gaining power with every kill."

Sam stiffened.

"This ritual... it was performed. By your father. I know you can't remember it, but it happened."

Her breath caught.

"But something went wrong," Raincloud continued. "During the ceremony, the spirit your father called upon looked at you instead of him. It made eye contact with you, and that's when everything changed."

Sam stood frozen.

"The spirit entered you, not him. And because it didn't fully merge with your father, he was left stuck, half man, half skinwalker. Incomplete. And you... You were left carrying the spirit's essence inside you. Not possessed, not consumed, but connected."

Raincloud took a breath, his tone firm but gentle now.

"I know this is hard to hear. But you must understand it. Because that spirit, the one inside you, it's going to try to convince you. To surrender. To let it take over."

He stepped closer, his eyes grave.

"If you give in, Rebekka... you won't exist anymore. Not as yourself. And that's something we cannot allow. Do you understand?"

Raincloud steps back, away from Sam, the stern and serious look fades from his face, back to a stern yet peaceful look.

At the same time, Detective Rogers walked down the hill towards Raincloud and Sam, who were resting near a stone wall structure. Rogers saw Sam sitting on the stone wall and recognized her from Fresno. Sam looked over, saw Rogers, and rolled her eyes. Rogers smiled politely at Sam, who returned a half-hearted, sarcastic smile.

Rogers adjusted his attention from Sam over to Raincloud.

"I thought that might be you. How've you been? It's been a long time, friend."

Raincloud gave a knowing smile, his eyes scanning Rogers like he was reading something more than just the man in front of him.

"It has been a long time, white man. You're not in Oregon anymore. I often wondered what path you took. Looks like Fresno's been feeding you well," he said, tapping his own stomach with a quiet laugh.

Rogers chuckled, rubbing his belly.

"Yeah, just a little soft around the edges these days. You, though, you haven't changed a bit. That strange medicine of yours must be doing something right."

Raincloud's smile lingered, but it didn't quite reach his eyes.

They exchanged a bit more small talk, the kind that dances around deeper things. Eventually, Raincloud's tone shifted.

"So," he said slowly, "why are you in Connecticut?"

Rogers's smile faded. He nodded toward Sam, who had drifted a short distance away, arms folded, back turned.

"I'm here because of her."

He hesitated, then pressed on.

"We closed her case a while back. The guy involved, he ended up dead in a way that didn't make a lick of sense. Looked almost ritualistic. Then I got assigned to another case out west... and damn if it wasn't nearly identical. The way the bodies were left, the symbols, the whole feel of it. It gave me that same cold crawl up my spine I used to get when we worked those weird cases in Oregon."

Raincloud didn't move. Didn't blink.

"I'm not saying she's involved," Rogers added quickly. "Not at all. But it made me dig deeper. And what I found was... well, about twenty years ago, there were two murders here in Connecticut. Same pattern. Almost to the letter."

He paused, rubbing the back of his neck.

"So I flew out, met with the guy who handled those old cases. Smart. Still sharp. We laid it all out, compared everything. And I swear to you,

317

Raincloud, if not for the twenty-year gap, I'd say we're looking at the same damn killer."

Raincloud's brow furrowed, his expression turning unreadable.

"Rogers... there's more to this than you can see."

Rogers tilted his head, suddenly cautious.

"More? Like what?"

Raincloud looked past him, to where Sam stood near the edge of the clearing, wind brushing her hair.

"I can't say. Not without her permission. She's the reason I'm here, too."

Rogers waited, uneasy now.

"My guides have shown me signs," Raincloud continued. "There is purpose in this. You didn't come here on instinct. I didn't either. This crossing of paths, it was set long ago, before either of us drew breath."

He turned his gaze back to Rogers.

"This isn't a coincidence. It's design. And you've stepped into something old, and very awake."

Rogers leaned against the stone wall, steam rising from the travel mug of diner coffee in his hand. Across from him stood Raincloud, leaning on the picnic table like he had all the time in the world.

"You remember Devil's Hollow?" Raincloud asked.

Rogers chuckled without humor. "How could I forget? My first homicide as lead detective. I still have dreams about that place."

Raincloud nodded slowly. "You weren't supposed to solve that one."

"That's what they told me at the station," Rogers replied, taking a sip of the coffee. "They thought I was in over my head. But you were there."

"I was," Raincloud said. "Because I knew something was off from the beginning. A girl disappears near tribal land, search dogs go scared, and the forest stays quiet for three days straight? That wasn't normal."

"You didn't tell me that at the time."

"I didn't think you'd believe me then. Hell, I barely believed it myself."

Rogers looked down at the worn grip of his sidearm. "And the ash?" he asked.

Raincloud reached into the leather pouch hanging from his belt and handed over a smaller, hand-stitched bag. It was soft and warm to the touch.

"White ash," Raincloud said. "From lightning-struck cottonwood. You dip your bullets in it. Not for killing people, don't ever use it for that. But if you're going to be facing something that doesn't die easily, this will slow it down."

Rogers turned the pouch over in his palm. "You saying we're about to face something like Devil's Hollow again?"

Raincloud didn't answer right away. Instead, he looked out past the tree line where Sam had wandered off to be alone. "That girl's carrying more than pain, Buk. Something ancient, something hungry. It's not the first time I've seen it. But it might be the last if we screw this up."

"You really think I'll need this?" Rogers asked, holding the pouch like it might burn him.

Raincloud met his eyes. "I think if you don't have it when the time comes, you won't survive.

And worse, you'll become what you're trying to stop."

Rogers slid the pouch into his coat pocket, the weight of it somehow heavier than it looked. He didn't say thank you. It didn't seem right to.

Sam walked back over, her eyes flicking to Rogers.

"So, what's Detective Rogers been telling you about me? Hope it's all glowing reviews."

Her tone was half-jest, half-probe, just enough sarcasm to mask the tension she felt radiating off both men.

Raincloud reached out and gently took her hand. "Rebekka," he said softly, "I'd like to bring Detective Rogers into the circle. He's chasing cases that cross paths with what we're facing. My guides say this meeting was not chance. He was sent here, to us. If we're to stand against what's coming, we must all walk the same path. But it's your choice. I do nothing without your permission."

Sam looked down at his weathered hand in hers, then gave it a gentle pat.

"I know you'd never move against me, Raincloud.

Like a father, you've always looked out for me. I trust you. And your instincts."

Raincloud gave a small nod.

"Thank you for that trust, Rebekka."

He kept hold of her hand but shifted, the other hand rising to the small leather pouch around his neck. His eyes closed as he began to whisper under his breath, a low murmuring in a language that felt older than the trees. His face tightened. He jerked once. Then again.

Suddenly, he released her hand, clapping his own together, fist into palm, with a sharp sound that cracked through the quiet.

His eyes snapped open.

"It stirs," he said, voice grave. "It watches."

He looked from Sam to Rogers.

"It doesn't know where we are… not yet. But it knows we're close. The veil is thinning. We must move now, go to the place where it lives."

He stepped back and motioned toward the cars. "We travel in separate vehicles. It may only sense Rebekka and me. Rogers, follow, but not too close.

If it doesn't know you're involved, that may give us an edge."

Rogers gave a short nod.

"I'll hang back, but not far."

Sam hesitated. Her gaze moved to Raincloud, then to Rogers. Her voice dropped.

"This place we're going... It's going to stir things in me. Things I've kept buried. If I start to slip, if something comes back... don't let it take hold."

Rogers met her eyes.

"You've got people watching your back now."

She gave him a small, somber smile.

"For what it's worth, be careful, Detective."

He tipped an imaginary hat.

"Always am."

Rogers turned and walked to his car.

Chapter 14 - Devils Hollow

Some fifteen years earlier, on the Grande Rhode
Reservation, a strange case unfolded before a newly
promoted Detective Buk Rogers and tribal elder and
guide, Raincloud.

A young girl named Angela Morningstar
vanished after attending a community powwow near
a place called Devil's Hollow, a small wooded
ravine on the edge of the reservation, long believed
to be cursed. Locals whispered of "the one who
waits beneath the stones."

Detective Buk Rogers of the Springfield,
Oregon Police Department was assigned the case. It
was high priority, but needed to stay low profile.
Angela was the daughter of a sitting state senator.
The case's political sensitivity required someone
who could "cut through the superstition." Rogers, a
no-nonsense officer with a clean record, was
chosen.

He believed this was most likely just a lost child
or a runaway. So, he did things by the book. He
brought in a canine unit to track the girl's last

known whereabouts using her hat and scarf. While the dogs began their work, Rogers focused on gathering witness statements.

The first two witnesses, friends of Angela, claimed they saw her walk off with someone, but when they looked back moments later, she was still walking, but alone. The person they thought they saw was tall, thin, and had unnaturally long arms. A third witness said Angela had been alone the entire time and was seen walking down toward the lower wooded ravine.

Rogers contacted the local sheriff and the liaison officer to the reservation, hoping for additional support or resources. He was told there were no extra officers to spare. Cases like this were "common" on the reservation, he was told. Teens often ran off, sometimes they returned, sometimes they didn't. The prevailing theory: Angela had likely run away to escape her father's overprotective grip. Rogers had already been warned not to expect much help from the locals. So far, that warning was holding true.

Meanwhile, the dog teams were coming up with nothing. The dogs either couldn't catch a scent, or refused to follow the one they found. Rogers was told some of the tracking electronics had malfunctioned in the field or gone completely dead. He was starting to feel that something more than procedural failure was at play. That feeling doubled when Raincloud showed up.

Rogers had worked with Raincloud on several past investigations involving Native land. He trusted the elder's instincts. In fact, he couldn't recall a time Raincloud had ever been wrong.

Raincloud had been called in at the request of Angela's grandmother. Rogers remembered something Raincloud once told him during their first case together:

"If you don't believe in the old stories, at least respect them. This land remembers things people forgot."

Rogers had never forgotten those words.

They contacted a local rancher whose land bordered the reservation and Devil's Hollow. They asked if she had any game cameras in the area, and if so, whether she could send the footage from the night Angela vanished. Later that afternoon, Rogers received the footage by email.

He forwarded through the file, then slowed it down around the time Angela was last seen leaving the community grounds. Two minutes into the slow-motion playback, they saw a girl, presumably Angela, walking a narrow path into the woods. A tall, shadowy figure followed her, its limbs abnormally long, its features eerily inhuman.

Rogers and Raincloud watched until the pair disappeared into the ravine.

Then Rogers rewound the footage to review it again, but this time, the strange figure was gone. Angela appeared to be walking alone.

He looked over at Raincloud, who had been silently watching from the edge of the desk. Rogers was shaken. "What did I just see… or not see?"

Raincloud nodded solemnly.
"The land remembers what man has forgotten."

Rogers didn't fully understand what that meant. But deep down, he knew it would matter, sooner or later.

Raincloud later told Rogers they would need to perform a ritual to find Angela, a ceremony that would allow them to see where she had gone. But it had to be done in Devil's Hollow itself.

Rogers wasn't thrilled with the idea. But he insisted on being present for the vision. He had to see whether Angela was alive or dead. Raincloud tried to dissuade him, warning that the ritual could be disturbing. Still, Rogers refused to back down.

"I can't tell you what you'll see," Raincloud said. "Visions are different for each person. Your first trance can be... very unsettling."

They trekked into Devil's Hollow together. Raincloud handed Rogers the tent poles while he carried the skin. Unsure of what was coming, Rogers joked,

"Raincloud, as a peace officer, I'm not sure I should ingest any kind of... uh... herbs. Exotic herbs. If you catch my meaning."

Raincloud only offered a slight smile. Rogers wasn't sure what to make of it.

They walked in silence down into the ravine. "Here," Raincloud said, stopping. "We set up the tent here."

Raincloud laid out the tent skin and instructed Rogers where to place the poles. Within minutes, the tent was assembled, and a fire pit crackled at the center. Raincloud pulled a long, carved pipe from his pack and packed it with a dark blend of tobacco or herbs, Rogers couldn't tell.

Raincloud removed his shoes and asked Rogers to do the same. Inside the tent, Raincloud stood on one side of the fire, motioning for Rogers to sit opposite him.

The sun had begun to set, casting long shadows outside the tent.

"We begin the Shaking Tent Ceremony," Raincloud announced.

He lit the pipe, began smoking, and started chanting, or was it singing? Rogers wasn't sure. Smoke filled the tent, heavy and sweet. Raincloud danced around the pit, occasionally blowing smoke directly into Rogers' face.

Rogers coughed, unsure what to do.

"Breathe it in," Raincloud instructed. "Let it fill your lungs. Close your eyes and focus on Angela. Don't think about me, don't listen to my voice. Listen for others. Look for her in the darkness behind your eyes."

Rogers inhaled. The smoke was sweet on his tongue and burned slightly in his nose. He tried to tune out everything, Raincloud, the fire, the sounds, and think only of Angela.

Then the noise faded. The scent vanished. And when Rogers opened his eyes, he was no longer in the tent.

He sat outside, alone. The stars above him blazed more brightly than he had ever seen. Angela appeared before him, scared, mute, reaching out. He couldn't touch her. He could see the fear in her eyes. She screamed silently.

Then came the voices, disembodied, whispering to him, showing him a path through Devil's Hollow. The vision zigged and zagged through trees and up steep hills before coming to a sudden halt that made his mind spin.

Then a white fox emerged from the underbrush and sat in front of him, locking eyes with his.

The world twisted, and Rogers collapsed.

"Rogers, Rogers, wake up!" Raincloud's voice pulled him back. Water splashed on his face.

Rogers opened his eyes slowly. His head throbbed like he'd taken a frying pan to the skull.

"Did you find her?" Raincloud asked. "Did the spirits show you where she is?"

"Yeah… I think so," Rogers replied, dazed. "That was… weird. Real weird."

Raincloud had already packed up the tent, put out the fire, and cleaned the site while Rogers lay unconscious.

Three days later, they found Angela, confused, dehydrated, but unharmed.

She described being "in the Hollow," where the sky never changed and the trees never moved. "It was like time was frozen," she said.

When asked to draw what she saw, Angela sketched a dark figure with red eyes, but no distinct form.

Rogers thanked Raincloud.

"I did nothing but show you the door," Raincloud replied. "The spirit guides led you to her. You're connected now, to the land and the spirit world. Like I am. Call me if you ever need help again. Or if you see something you can't explain."

Rogers gave him a nod and a small smile. "Will do, Raincloud."

Then he tipped an invisible hat and returned to Springfield.

He closed the case, listing the cause of disappearance as "exposure and temporary disorientation."

But Rogers knew better.

The case had changed him. He was no longer certain what he believed, but he knew now that anything was possible.

Especially when it came to the things that walked between worlds.

Chapter 15 - The Confrontation

Sam and Raincloud climbed into the silver Rogue and pulled away, the road ahead stretching toward whatever waited at the edge of memory and shadow.

The narrow road to the commune closed in around them, trees arching overhead like silent sentinels. Shadows stretched long despite the afternoon light, their branches clawing at the Rogue's windows. Sam's fingers tightened around the door handle.

She could feel her memories stirring, or something that wore the shape of memory. *Were they mine? Or were they being fed to me?* Reality thinned.

"The trees..." she muttered. "They're watching us. I know that sounds crazy, but something's not right. My sight's off, Raincloud. I'm seeing things that aren't real. Or maybe they are. I can't tell."

Raincloud reached across the console and gently pressed her eyelids shut. "Keep them closed, Rebekka. The spirit is twisting your vision, showing you sacred things, but warped. Blended with your past. I'll call on my guides to protect you, to help you see true."

With her eyes closed, the world around her softened to sounds: gravel under tires, the low hum of the engine, the breath of the wind slipping through the trees.

But Raincloud felt it too, eyes on them. Not from the woods. From behind windows. Behind doors. The commune was still as death. No children. No dogs. No voices. The people inside knew something had awakened in the forest, and they'd shuttered their lives in fear. They had lived with it for twenty years. Long enough to know when to hide.

Behind them, Rogers followed at a cautious distance, just close enough to keep visual. Years of surveillance made it second nature. But this, this wasn't his usual territory. Spirits. Visions. Skinwalkers. He wasn't prepared for any of it. Still, he trusted Raincloud. He had to. He glanced again at the photographs in the passenger seat, holding one up to the window, trying to match tree lines and ridges. Nothing quite aligned.

"*Welcome home, Rebekka. I've missed you. Soon we will be together.*"

Sam's breath caught. The voice wasn't in her ears. It was *inside*. Her pulse spiked. She could hear the tires crunching gravel, feel the car in motion. She was awake. This was happening.

"Stop!" she snapped. "We're here."

Raincloud hit the brakes. The Rogue rocked to a halt. He turned to her, voice low. "What is it, Rebekka? What do you feel?"

"He's here. The spirit... it's talking to me again. I *feel* him. Not just inside. He's close, physically close. Breathing distance. What do I do?"

Her voice quivered, on the edge of panic. She wasn't just hearing it anymore. She was *sensing* it, inside her bones.

Then came a shift. New images flickered behind her eyes, but this time they weren't from the spirit. They were someone else's eyes. A second sight. She saw trees. Brambles. Overgrown brush. A rusted truck hidden beneath years of vines. Her heart skipped.

"My dad's truck," she whispered. "The old log hauler. It's here. I *see* it."

Raincloud looked but saw only thickets.

Sam opened her eyes, just a sliver. Trees. Weeds. Nothing else. She closed them again, and the truck returned, gleaming in her mind. Just past it stood an old white frame house. Weather-worn. Familiar. *Home.*

The fire pit was still there. She could almost hear the laughter of cousins, the crackle of burning cedar, the taste of marshmallows singed on the edge.

Raincloud killed the engine. Silence wrapped around them.

"This is the place," he said softly. "This is where it lives."

He could feel his guides rising like heat from the earth. Warning him. Be alert. Be ready. Not everything you see can be trusted. But he would follow Rebekka's vision. Even into the dark.

"My guides are your eyes now, Rebekka," Raincloud said softly. "We follow them. They won't let the spirit lead you astray. Stay put, I'll come get you."

He stepped out of the Rogue, the gravel crunching beneath his boots. Up the road, he spotted Rogers' vehicle. A quick nod passed between them; Rogers shifted his car into park and waited.

Raincloud circled to the passenger side and opened Sam's door.

"It's me, Rebekka," he said gently. "I'm going to place my bandana over your eyes. It'll force you to rely on the vision of the spirit guides. Don't fight it."

From his back pocket, he pulled a worn red bandana and tied it snugly around her head, covering her eyes.

"Try opening your eyes. Can you see anything?"

Sam's fingers brushed the fabric. "Uh… no. Just black."

"Good." Raincloud knelt beside her, close enough that his voice dropped to a whisper. "Reach your arm out and find my shoulder."

339

She reached hesitantly, her hand grazing the fabric of his shirt, then trailing up his sleeve until she found his shoulder and gripped it.

"Got it."

Raincloud rose, and Sam followed his motion, stepping carefully out of the car. He closed the door quietly behind her.

He scanned the tree line ahead. Thick brush, tall grass, gnarled branches.

"What do you see, Rebekka?" he asked.

Sam tilted her head slightly. Her breath hitched. "I see… a white logging truck. My dad's. Parked right there." Sam pointed to a place she could see, but Raincloud saw nothing but growth. "Past that, there's a fire pit made of stone. We used to roast game, marshmallows… play there. And beyond it, a house. White wood siding. Sagging porch. Three windows in front. A screen door that always slammed shut."

Raincloud narrowed his eyes, trying to cut through the tangle of green and brown. Nothing. Then, just barely, a glint. A sliver of rusted chrome, maybe a bumper.

"Do you see anything else?" he asked. "Any figure? Animal, human, anything watching?"

"Not yet." Her voice was small. Tense.

Then a voice slid through her mind. "He isn't welcome here."

Sam flinched. "Raincloud," she whispered, "he says you're not wanted here."

Raincloud stood taller, unmoved. His tone sharpened, cutting the air. "That's fine, Rebekka. I'm not going anywhere."

Rogers could still see Sam and Raincloud up ahead, disappearing into the overgrown brush just beyond the car. As the last glimpse of them slipped out of sight, he cut the engine and stepped out, easing the door closed behind him.

He glanced around. The few nearby homes looked lived-in, but the yards were empty. No one outside. Still, he had the feeling he was being watched, shadows shifting behind curtains, eyes tucked just out of sight.

He pulled out the old photographs from Kirby's case file, trying once more to line them up with the landscape. Nothing matched exactly. Too much time had passed, weather, decay, the slow reclaiming of everything by nature.

Keeping his instincts sharp, Rogers started toward the spot where Sam and Raincloud had gone. He hadn't made it more than seventy feet from the car when he heard a voice. A woman's voice. Not Sam. Not Raincloud.

He turned, scanning the street.

A woman was crossing the road toward him, walking from one of the houses. Middle-aged, maybe a little older. She raised a hand and wagged a finger at him. "Hey! You don't want to go wandering into them woods."

Rogers took a slow step back toward the road, hands open and visible. "That right? You from around here?"

"You here with the city? Or lake commission?" The lady walked a bit closer towards Rogers.

She was close enough now that he could tell she wasn't carrying anything. Her eyes, though, they were sharp and watchful. He kept his tone light. "No, ma'am. Just visiting. Came down to look at some lots near Cedar Lake. Figured I'd check out the area."

She narrowed her eyes. "You ain't no tourist. You're a cop."

Rogers offered a half-smile. "That obvious?"

"I see your kind. Seen plenty." She gave him a knowing smirk. "I'm Mrs. Custer."

"Well, Mrs. Custer, you got me. I'm here on official business, trying to match some case photos to the area. Would you maybe be able to help."

He pulled out two of the cleaner photos, no bodies, and held them up. "Recognize the spot?"

She leaned in, eyes flicking over them. "Those're old. Twenty years, maybe. That's the place just down there." She pointed in the direction Sam and Raincloud had gone. "Back of the property, where the brush gets thick. No one lives there now. Ain't been anyone since that woman and her baby were found..."

Her voice drifted. Her face darkened.

"They never found the man," she added, quieter. "No one touches that land. Won't even walk on the same side of the street. People say it's cursed. Bad medicine."

Rogers nodded, absorbing it all. "You seen anyone out there recently? Any strange activity?"

She shook her head hard. "No one goes near it. Not unless they're asking for trouble."

"Well, I guess I'm asking," Rogers said. "But if I'm not back in an hour or two, maybe send someone looking. Or call it in."

Mrs. Custer glanced at the brush, then back at him. "Okay," she said. "But don't go dying over there, officer."

She hesitated.

"'Cause you might not stay dead."

Rogers offered a tight smile, thanked her, and turned back toward the brush where Sam and Raincloud had disappeared.

Detective Rogers moved down the road to where he saw Raincloud and Sam entered the brush. He stepped into the thick growth, his boots crunching softly against the pine needles and brittle undergrowth. The trees here grew closer together, their branches knitting tightly overhead, filtering what little daylight remained. The light was fading fast. Too fast. The deeper he walked, the more he felt it, like the forest was shrinking in around him, warping slightly at the edges.

The trail should've led him straight to where Raincloud and Sam were. He felt like he was walking in a different direction, like the woods were forcing him in circles.

Rogers stopped. He turned slowly in a full circle. Nothing looked familiar. The wind had died down completely, and the woods had gone still. Too still. Then he saw it, out of the corner of his eye, movement. Something hunched and low slipped between the trees.

"Raincloud?" he whispered reflexively, though he already knew it wasn't him.

He drew in a breath and walked forward, eyes scanning the forest floor and the shifting shadows between trees. A chill slipped under his coat.

That's when the air thickened. Like walking into water.

And just ahead, where he swore there'd been a clearing before, there was now only dense underbrush. Tangled branches, thorn-choked paths, bramble where there had been none. Rogers narrowed his eyes and pushed forward, brushing back a thick limb.

Then he saw it, or didn't.

The house.

For a split second, it was there: the old one Raincloud had mentioned. Weathered wood. A sagging porch. Curtains blowing in windows where no glass remained.

And just as quickly, it vanished. Like a mirage dissolving in heat.

Rogers stood still. A low, guttural growl echoed somewhere behind him.

He didn't turn right away. He kept his voice low. "You're not hiding it from me forever."

A branch cracked.

Then silence.

He backed away slowly, hand resting near the grip of his sidearm, not out of threat, but instinct.

By the time he found the path again, sweat clung to his neck despite the cold. Behind him, the woods looked exactly as they should. Untouched. Quiet. Innocent.

But Rogers knew better now.

Something in that forest *didn't want the house to be found.*

And it was still watching him.

***

Sam felt disoriented, not blind, but not seeing through her own eyes either. It was more like drifting between two overlapping visions: one tethered to the present, the other soaked in memory. The white logging truck. The blackened fire pit. The house. She recognized them, but they pulsed in and out of focus like echoes from a half-forgotten dream.

"We need to go to the house," she whispered.

Raincloud grunted softly beside her. "You can speak openly now. The spirit knows we're here." His voice lowered. "But don't mention Rogers. It doesn't know there's a third."

Sam placed a hand on his shoulder. "It's this way, toward the porch." She nudged him gently.

Raincloud followed her lead, though he saw nothing but thickets and trees. "There's nothing here, Rebekka. The house... I don't think it exists anymore."

"No," Sam said, voice urgent. "I can *see* it, in the spirit vision. It's here."

She pulled him forward a single step.

The air shifted. Trees thinned. Brush peeled away. The house revealed itself, abruptly and unnaturally, as if dropping its disguise.

Raincloud paused on the porch. Something felt wrong. The house looked pristine, too clean, too untouched. His skin prickled.

"The spirit's stronger than I thought," he said, voice tight. "It's clouding my sight."

He closed his eyes and yanked the pouch from his neck. Gripping it, he whispered a prayer. When he opened his eyes again, the illusion dissolved.

Now he saw the truth: a decaying husk of a home, roof sagging, limbs choking its frame. Yet something had been living here. Recently.

"The skinwalker still resides here," he said.

Sam stiffened. Her throat went dry, but she nodded. "I see the house... the one the spirit wants me to see. But not the signs you're seeing."

Raincloud stepped forward. The front wall was gone, either rotted away or ripped open. There was no threshold anymore, just a gaping mouth into darkness.

"Do you see anything?" Raincloud asked, eyes sharp.

Sam squinted, reaching for something buried. "I don't know. Maybe in the hallway... or the den. There's something there. I think I remember..."

She didn't. Not fully. But something pressed against her mind, a presence waiting to be named.

She guided Raincloud deeper into the house. The floor groaned beneath their weight. Raincloud moved carefully, helping her step around holes in the wood. Sam scanned the den, heart pounding. Then she saw it.

"The spirit," she whispered. "It's here. In the corner."

Raincloud turned, nothing. Just shadows and rot.

He closed his eyes and called to the guides.

When he looked again, it was there.

Not smoke. Not shadow.

A *thing*, half-man, half-nightmare. Crimson eyes locked on him. A mouth too wide, filled with too many teeth.

"Back," Raincloud barked, shoving Sam toward the porch. His instincts screamed trap. "They wanted us *inside*. This whole place is a lure."

Something moved behind them.

The den sighed. And the floor creaked, not under them, but under *something else*.

Raincloud resisted the urge to turn back toward the door.

"No," Sam said. "Something isn't right. I see smoke… and you see a skinwalker. Why are we seeing two different things?"

Raincloud froze.

"Raincloud," she whispered, "I think there's something behind us."

She glanced once more toward the corner, the smoke-shadow still hung there, but it flickered now, like a candle guttering in a breeze.

"It's not real," Sam said. "Whatever's behind us... *that's* what's real."

Together, slowly, they turned.

Down the hallway, something moved, low to the ground, crawling. Its limbs were too long, elbows jutting at wrong angles, claws tapping against the rotting floorboards with a delicate rhythm that sounded like mockery.

It didn't look human. It didn't look animal. It looked like a nightmare that had never learned the rules of the waking world.

Sam tried desperately to see her father's face in the beast, but there was no recognition, not even in the eyes. "Daddy, it's Sam, your daughter. Don't you remember me at all? The beast only growled, its eyes flashing red, and stepped closer to Sam and Raincloud.

"He belongs to me. Your dear father doesn't exist, just as you and your medicine man will not exist before our meeting is over, Rebekka." The dark voice hissed in her mind. Sam took a step back towards Raincloud. She knew that skinwalker beast was part of her father. It was fully beast, and if they

351

let it combine with the essence spirit, then neither she, Raincloud, or Rogers would make it through the confrontation.

Raincloud narrowed his eyes. In all his years walking the shadow path, he'd never encountered a spirit or beast like this. It wasn't a skinwalker, not like the ones from the old stories. This was *older*. *Wrong in every sense.*

He could feel the spirit guides behind him, gathering, but he knew, they weren't enough. Not for this.

If they were going to survive, he and Rebekka would need something much more powerful.

Sam's vision began to flicker, shifting between reality and something darker, unreal. Her knees buckled. A wave of dizziness hit her, but it didn't feel like faintness, it felt like something was *taking over*.

Her eyes rolled back, and she collapsed. Raincloud caught her just before she hit the floor.

"Rebekka?" he whispered.

But she was gone.

The spirit guides in his mind were dim, muffled, as though retreating. He was alone now, with only his eyes, his wits, and what he could call upon.

Then Sam stood.

She rose slowly, her posture wrong, her movements fluid but unnatural. Raincloud looked into her face and saw no trace of Rebekka. Her eyes had turned white, her expression twisted and cold.

She slid her hand along Raincloud's cheek, then curled it slowly around his neck. Her grin split into something cruel, ancient.

Then she turned from him and walked toward the nightmare beast crouched at the end of the hall.

"Hello, Daddy…" she said with a gravelly chuckle. "You waited a long time, but the wait is over."

She turned back to Raincloud, eyes burning white.

"You never saw this coming, did you, old man?" she sneered. "What a blind little medicine man you are. Sweet Rebekka is going to be sacrificed, finally. The ritual that started so many years ago? It ends *tonight*."

She took a step closer, her smile curving like a blade.

"And you? You're going to watch. Then your blood will be the *first*, first of many, to usher in our true form. Our *completed* form."

Raincloud didn't flinch. He straightened, his grip tightening around the medicine pouch in his hand.

Sam's body moved in sharp bursts, too fast, too precise, lunging at him with a strength that didn't belong to her. Raincloud deflected, turning her momentum away, never striking, but each blow she delivered rattled his bones. He could smell the musk of wild animal on her skin, see the twitching in her fingers where claws *wanted* to be.

He began the chant, low and steady, each word like a stone laid in the path to drive the spirit out. Sam flinched at the sound, but the thing inside her laughed, a guttural, mocking sound that echoed from somewhere far deeper than her lungs.

"Your words are dust. She's mine now."

"You are not what you pretend to be, spirit," he said, voice steady. "You puff your chest, speak your poison, but your words are hollow. Your power is only in that half-beast behind you. I know your limits, spirit, and I know truths you do not."

His eyes gleamed as he took a step forward, voice rising, shaking the air between them. Sam's movements grew more frantic, jerking as if pulled by invisible strings. Her nails raked the side of his cheek, drawing blood, and for a heartbeat the world swam, he saw visions: cedar trees bending in a storm, the dark mouth of a cave, and inside it, eyes like molten rubies watching him.

He staggered, but the song in his chest did not falter.

Raincloud ended his chant then looked into the eyes of the spirit. "My words are true. And they carry the honor of my ancestors."

Raincloud reached into the pouch, pulled out ash, herbs, bits of bone. He tossed the contents high, the mixture shimmering as it scattered in the air.

Sam's body jerked. The skinwalker beast took several lurching steps back. Something in the smoke hissed.

Raincloud's eyes locked on Sam.

The spirit shrieked through her, the sound making the air shimmer. Her face changed if only for a second, then the evil grin returned.

But the *thing* behind Sam recoiled, and in that instant, *the skinwalker creature and the spirit* saw something neither expected.

All Sam could see was darkness.

She knew this place. The spirit's place.
It was where it brought her in dreams and visions, over and over again.
Only now, she understood, this wasn't just a dream. The spirit had taken control. It had *locked her away* in here.

She screamed into the void. Stomped her feet. Nothing changed. No echo, no resistance. Just thick, swallowing black.

Think, Sam. Think.

She slowed her breathing, tried to listen. Maybe she could tune into something, anything, outside of this prison.
There. A sound. Voices. Muffled. Distant.
Distorted. She realized one of them was *hers*, but

warped and wrong, a mockery of her voice, speaking with someone else's malice.

Then she heard him. Raincloud.

She couldn't make out the words, but it was *him*. And at the end of his voice, something happened.

A flicker. The darkness rippled. The spirit *shuddered*. It almost lost control.

Sam's heart leapt. Raincloud didn't know she was in here, but if he did, maybe he could break the spirit's grip. She had to reach him, somehow. Show him she was still inside.

There had to be a way. Her mind reached, searching. Then she remembered the drawing table.

The spirit had put it here before… a trick to keep her quiet, distracted. But if it created it, maybe *she* could summon it now. Use it *against* the spirit.

She closed her eyes and focused.

Come on, Sam. Picture it. Focus on the table.

A glow sparked behind her eyelids. Faint at first, like the first hint of sunrise through thick fog. She opened her eyes.

There it was. The drawing table.

Dimly lit by the little green lamp she remembered. Pencils, charcoal, paper, waiting.

She rushed to the seat, hands trembling as she grabbed a pencil.

"This has to work," she whispered, breath sharp. "If the spirit can draw, then so can I. I can reach them."

And she began to draw, feverishly, desperately.

Not pictures of dreams this time. Not visions of the past.

Messages.

Words. Symbols. Shapes that meant something, ancient and real.

Something the spirit wouldn't understand until it was too late.

Sam's grin twisted wider, a grotesque mimic of joy.

"A little magic pouch, eh, medicine man? Is that all you have?" Her voice dripped with mockery.

"You really think my words hold no power, old man?"

She quickly thrust her hand forward with a flick of her wrist, like shoving the very air.

Raincloud didn't see it coming.

It hit him like an invisible freight train, hurling him across the room. He slammed into the crumbling remains of a rotted wall, boards snapping under the impact, before collapsing to the floor in a heap. The air whooshed out of his lungs.

Gasping, he rolled to his side, pushing himself up to hands and knees.
His body ached, but his eyes stayed locked on her. Steady.
Unshaken.

He rose to his feet, brushing off the dust and grit from his clothes. His eyes were still locked on Sam. The pouch lay at his feet. He reached down for the leather pouch that had slipped from his fingers.

Sam raised her arm again. Another push.
The pouch skittered across the floor, spinning out of reach, disappearing into the shadows of the back room.

Raincloud didn't flinch. He looked her dead in the eye, gaze unmoving, and also stared beyond her, at the *thing* coiled behind her in the veil of darkness.

359

"You see that?" Sam laughed, dark joy rippling in her tone. "Is *that* not power, medicine man?"

"I could've sent you through that wall, shattered every bone in your body. But we need you alive. You'll be the first blood sacrifice once we're one. You'll watch it all burn. You'll *see* what fear really is."

Her voice changed, becoming deeper, older. A layering of voices.

"Your ancestors feared me long ago. But this time... there'll be no return. No sealing me away. We will tear through this world."

Raincloud's eyes narrowed. His brow creased in concentration.

"I don't need my pouch to defeat you," he said quietly.

His stance shifted. He drew in a deep breath.

"If that's all the power you have... You don't have *enough*."

Raincloud reached his arms out and brought them crashing together with a sound like thunder tearing the sky in half. A shockwave roared through the rotting house, the walls groaning in protest as dust, splinters, and long-forgotten cobwebs spun through the air like ash in a storm.

From the rippling air, shapes began to form, ghostlike at first, then solid with the weight of history. White and blue figures of light stepped forward, their feet making no sound as they crossed the ruined floor. Medicine men, warriors, and spirit guides from across the ages, Raincloud's own bloodline, entered the narrow space between him and the thing wearing Sam's skin.

The skinwalker inside her recoiled, its white gaze narrowing. It leaned forward like a predator sniffing the wind, trying to place the scent of power it had not encountered in centuries.

Then, without warning, the ancestral spirits surged forward. Spears of light clashed with the beast's hooked claws, each impact ringing like struck stone. The air filled with the sound of battle, howls and roars mixing with the deep, resonant hum of the spirits' war songs. It was a sound the commune had never heard before and would never hear again.

The skinwalker lashed out, teeth bared, raking through the air at foes it could not quite touch, its body jerking as invisible wounds opened across its borrowed flesh. Still, it tried to force its body forward, to break through the line of spirits, but each step was pushed back, each strike met with another from the glowing warriors.

Through it all, Raincloud's voice never faltered. His chant rose and fell like the drumbeat of a storm.

Sam turned suddenly, not toward the spirits tearing at the beast, but toward Raincloud himself. Between them stood a single figure, motionless, robed in light older than stone. The air seemed to bow around him. The skinwalker spirit hesitated, almost instinctively lowering its eyes.

The spirit looked at Sam, not the beast, but the girl inside, and smiled. Then, in a slow unraveling, it dissolved into white smoke and drifting ash. The cloud swirled once before surging into Sam's mouth like a breath drawn in reverse.

The spirit howled, stumbling, its grip on her faltering. For the briefest heartbeat, its white gaze went dull, and Raincloud saw them. Sam's eyes. Human. Wide with fear, but alive.

That was all he needed.

Sam could hear the destruction happening outside her body, the clash of spirits, Raincloud's voice roaring like a storm, but she didn't stop drawing. The scratching of her pencil against the paper was frantic, desperate. This was the only way she could fight back, to use the spirit's own tools against it.

She clung to the drawing table as a thunderclap shook the space around her. Even inside this dark prison, she heard it. Felt it. The walls of shadow flickered like flame in the wind. The spirit felt it too, its grip faltered, if only for a moment.

Then, through the pulsing dark, she saw someone standing across the room.

Her breath caught. At first, she thought it was the spirit, coming to finish what it started. But no. His face wasn't twisted with hate or hunger. His eyes were hard and sharp, yet calm. Centered. Something ancient stirred behind them.

He crossed the space without a word and stopped beside her. His gaze dropped to the drawing.

Sam glanced at it, then back to the man. His presence was like stone, still, yet immense. When he placed a hand on her shoulder, she flinched at the touch. But there was no pain. Only warmth. With his other hand, he touched the drawing, turning the drawing into smoke, like burning paper. Sam recoiled slightly, thinking all that urgent work was gone until the man cupped the smoke with his hand and blew it into Sam's face. Sam inhaled the smoke. It felt as if there was something living in the smoke.

He closed his eyes and whispered words she couldn't understand. The sound was like wind through pine trees, faint but full of meaning. Then the wind became real.

A gale tore through the room, circling her. Spirits flew like leaves in a storm, voices echoing in languages long buried. Light shimmered in the darkness.

And then, silence.

The wind was gone. So was the spirit man.

Sam blinked. The drawing was gone from the table.

Something had changed. She couldn't explain it. Couldn't name it. But she felt it in her bones.

Raincloud watched as his spirit guides descended upon the skinwalker like a storm of light, striking again and again. The creature snarled and hissed, trying to back down the hall, clawing at the air as if trying to claw its way out of existence. Then, all at once, the guides surged forward, into Sam.

Her body convulsed violently, as if struck by lightning. Raincloud stepped forward, but just as quickly as the spirits had entered, they vanished.

What had they done?

He didn't know, but he trusted them. They had never led him astray. Not since he was a boy.

Sam's eyes flickered, white, blue, white again, then settled on pure white. Her grin returned, wider now, like a rip tearing across her face.

"So," the voice inside her said, low and curling, "you had more than medicine in your pouch, old man. It was... honorable. But a miserable failure. Your spirits are no match for an ancient such as I."

Raincloud watched her closely, knowing Sam herself was in there, hanging on by threads. But her gaze shifted, narrowing, predatory, staring at something beyond him.

Rogers.

Raincloud lunged at the opening, driving forward and slamming into her with everything he had. They hit the floor hard, boards cracking beneath them. He had nothing left, no words, no spirits, no time. Only Rogers could end this.

"ROGERS!" Raincloud roared, wrestling against her as her limbs writhed with serpentine strength. "In the hall! Use it! NOW!"

Sam's body convulsed, and then it was like wrestling smoke and steel at the same time. The thing inside her surged, skin stretching over muscles that weren't hers, bones shifting in subtle, impossible ways. Her head snapped toward him, and her mouth opened in a grin that was all teeth, no warmth.

She ripped herself free with a violent twist, throwing him like he weighed nothing. Raincloud slammed into the wall, ribs screaming. He barely had time to gasp before she was there, on him in a blur, one hand clamping around his throat, lifting him off the ground. Her nails bit deep, drawing blood.

Her breath was ice. Her eyes were fire. And somewhere deep inside, behind the glowing crimson, he thought he saw a flicker, Sam's own eyes, flaring in terror.

The spirit wanted her to watch him die.

From the hallway, *BAM. BAM-BAM-BAM.*

The beast screamed, its guttural howls split the air as Rogers emptied his clip into the skinwalker's true form.

Sam spun toward the noise, never releasing her grip on Raincloud. Her focus went from Rogers standing over the beast as it lay dead in the hallway back to Raincloud.

Raincloud's boots skidded across the warped floorboards as Sam's possessed body slammed him against the wall. Her grip was like iron, fingers crushing into his windpipe.

"You tested me and lost," the voice said through her lips, low, guttural, ancient. "Your ancestors spoke the language of life, and they died. You speak the language of death… and I grant it."

The hallway trembled under the force of the spirit's rage.

From somewhere deep inside, Sam was watching. Trapped in a hollow of her own mind, she saw Raincloud not as the man pinned against the wall, but as a blazing figure surrounded by the white-blue shimmer of his ancestors. They stood behind him, old men, warriors, healers, fading, their edges dissolving into mist. One by one, they pressed their hands to his back, merging their light into him.

The spirit inside her recoiled at the sight, its claws twitching. "This will not save you."

Raincloud's eyes locked on Sam's, not the beast's, but hers. Somehow, impossibly, he saw her. *Hold on,* his gaze said. *I walk this road so you don't have to.*

Her throat burned with a cry she couldn't make, watching helplessly as the spirit tightened its grip. Raincloud's boots left the floor. His breath came in choking rasps. Still, he didn't claw at her hands, he pressed his own palm against her chest, directly over her heart.

"You can't take her soul without taking mine first," he rasped, every word tearing from his lungs. Then his voice steadied, a note of calm breaking through the chaos. "And I give it freely."

Something broke loose in the air, Sam felt it as a sharp pull in her gut, a tearing. The spirit inside her lunged at him, not to fight but to feed. Its hunger was raw, feral, pulling the very light from Raincloud's body. His ancestors flared brighter for one last instant… and then went dark, their energy pouring into him until there was nothing left of them.

Raincloud's body jerked once, twice. The sound of bone splintering cracked through the hallway. The spirit leaned in close, almost whispering into his dying ear. Sam didn't hear the words, but she saw the smile on Raincloud's bloodied lips. He was ready.

The final twist came like thunder in her chest. She felt him go.

And for the briefest heartbeat, the spirit faltered.

Rogers was already moving. The white ash pouch in his hand as he charged, scattering the dust in a wide arc. The spirit screamed, not with rage, but with terror, its form peeling away from Sam's body in roiling waves of black and red.

First, one arm dropped to her side.

Then the other.

She tried to lift them, but they wouldn't obey.

And that's when the dragon tattoo on her shoulder *moved*.

The spirit inside her blinked, confused. The ink writhed, slithering down her shoulder, coiling around her arm, thickening. It shimmered, scaled, alive. The dragon's head reared up from her palm, glowing red eyes locked onto hers.

"What... what is this?" the spirit whispered. She turned to run, back to the hall, but Rogers was already there, standing guard, weapon raised.

The spirit's gaze darted between the front door and the hallway, calculating, desperate. The ash still burned in the air, searing against its essence, but it was the dragon that rooted it in place.

The ink shifted again, coils tightening up Sam's forearm, scales glinting like molten obsidian. The head lifted, lips peeling back to show needle-fine teeth. Heat radiated from it, blistering, and the air filled with the deep, resonant thrum of something older than the spirit itself.

"You... mimic," the spirit croaked through Sam's lips. "You were banished."

The Uktena spirit only tilted its head, as if amused. "I have waited," it said. Its voice wasn't loud, it was *inside* the walls, the floor, the marrow of Sam's bones. "Waited for you to crawl back into the world you abandoned. And now..." Its mouth widened into a smile that was all hunger. "...you've delivered yourself to me."

The spirit tried to force Sam's body backward, away from the arm, but each step was heavier than the last, as if the dragon's coils were tightening

371

around *its* legs, not hers. Black smoke peeled from her skin where the Uktena's scales touched.

Rogers didn't move. He knew what he was watching wasn't his fight anymore.

The spirit thrashed inside Sam, clawing for control, but the Uktena's eyes only flared brighter, locking onto its prey. "Run if you wish. I will catch you in this world… or the next."

It tried. It really tried, tearing itself from Sam's chest in a final, violent surge. The Uktena lunged. Its jaws snapped shut on the spirit's trailing essence, dragging it back, coiling around it in midair.

The scream that followed wasn't human. It wasn't animal. It was the sound of something being erased from the memory of the world.

When it ended, the Uktena's coils loosened, slithering back up Sam's arm and into place on her shoulder. The ink stilled. The scales became skin again.

Sam dropped to her knees, gasping for breath. Raincloud's body lay still against the wall. Rogers was already moving toward her, but her gaze was locked on the dragon's eyes, now quiet, yet still watching.

Silence settled heavy in the room.

Then Sam gasped again, her body jolting with sudden life. She blinked, her white eyes clearing to a bright, clear blue.

Her plan had worked.

The drawing she made of Uktena, merged with her own dragon tattoo, had come alive. Using the spirit-infused drawing table, she made the tattoo move, made it speak in her own voice. The spirit guides had answered, they'd merged Uktena with her, if only for a moment.

She sat up slowly, groggy, and then spotted Raincloud's crumpled form across the room, a Thunderbird feather lay by his head.

"No... no... no..." she whispered, voice cracking with grief.

Crawling forward, she laid trembling hands on his chest.

"Thank you, Raincloud," she said softly, tears tracing paths down her face. "You're at peace with your ancestors now...Sleep well, my friend."

For a moment, she rested her head on his chest. Then she jerked upright, alert and tense.

Rogers stepped forward cautiously, hands raised in peace.

"Hold on there, little lady. It's me, Detective Rogers. I think it's gone now."

Sam's wild eyes locked onto his.

"It's over," he said, voice cracking with emotion. "It's over, Sam."

He looked down at Raincloud, his old friend, and the weight of loss finally crashed down on him. Raincloud had told him he was meant to be a sacrifice for Sam, something Rogers had pushed away, unwilling to accept.

But now, there was no denying it.

***

At the Chester Memorial Hospital

The hospital lights were too bright.

Sam squinted against them, her arms wrapped tightly around her midsection like she had to hold herself together. A nurse passed by, but Sam barely noticed. Everything felt muffled, like sound underwater, like a dream she hadn't quite woken from.

The dragon tattoo on her arm was still there. But it looked different now, sharper, older. Sometimes, when she blinked too fast or too slow, she swore it moved.

On the table beside her sat a glass of ice water, a vase of white lilies, and a small note written in elegant script:

"*You're safe. Come back to us. , J.*" Sam read it three times.

At the doorway, Detective Rogers leaned against the frame, arms crossed. His usually easy posture was tense.

"Hey there, little lady—Sam," he said, voice softer than she'd ever heard it. "Glad to see you're awake. I wasn't exactly sure when that might happen. You were out for a while."

He stepped further into the room, rubbing the back of his neck. "I wanted to come by before I left for Fresno. Make sure you were okay. The doctors are calling it a stress-induced blackout, but… You and I both know it was more than that."

Sam looked down at her arm again, tracing the ink with her eyes. Then she glanced back at him. "So... what are you going to do about your open cases back in Fresno?"

Rogers exhaled slowly, shifting his weight as he looked out the window and back to her. "I honestly don't know. I can't exactly write up a report that says a shadow thing tried to eat our souls, and Raincloud sacrificed himself so you could live. Hell, the captain wouldn't believe a quarter of it. I'm not sure I even believe it, and I was there."

"For what it's worth…" Sam gave a tired smile, the first he'd seen from her. "I'm having a hard time with it, too. But I'm glad you were there. I couldn't have done it without you, or Raincloud."

Rogers cleared his throat, blinking hard. "Yeah… me too. It's strange. Hadn't seen him in years, but when we met at that rest stop, it was like no time had passed. Picked up right where we left off."

Sam nodded, her eyes glistening.

Rogers tipped an imaginary hat. "Well, I'll let you get some rest. Safe trip home."

He turned to leave.

"Detective Rogers," Sam called.

He stopped, turning his head back to the doorframe.

"Don't be a stranger. Maybe come by the shop sometime. I'll see if I can convince you to get a tattoo." Her smile warmed slightly. "Then you can tell me if it hurts or not."

Rogers chuckled. "I might just do that." He paused, looking at her one last time. "So long, kiddo."

He turned and walked down the hall, disappearing around the corner.

A day later, the door opened, and Dr. West stepped in. She looked tired, older, maybe, but her voice was soft. "Hello, Sam."

Sam didn't answer. Just looked at her hands.

Dr. West crossed the room slowly and sat at the edge of the bed. "You gave us all a hell of a scare."

"You knew," Sam finally whispered. "Didn't you? You knew it wasn't just trauma."

Dr. West hesitated. "I suspected. I wasn't sure how deep it went."

"You saw the shadows around me and still kept digging."

"I had to," she said. "You matter."

Sam nodded slowly, but her eyes glistened. "Raincloud is gone."

"I know."

"I killed him."

"No," Dr. West said, voice firmer. "The thing inside you did. He chose to help you. He knew the risk."

That broke something in Sam. Her lips trembled and she covered her face with both hands. "I don't know how to live with this."

"You're not alone," said a voice from the door.

Julie stood there, awkward, unsure, clutching a paper bag of takeout and a half dozen wildflowers in her other hand. She looked pale but determined.

"You came!" Sam said, a crack in her voice. "You came all the way here to see me."

"I brought your favorite," Julie said. "The one with too much garlic."

Sam managed a weak smile. "That one always made you gag."

"I'm making an exception," Julie said, stepping in.

Sam opened her arms like a child, and Julie rushed forward. They clung to each other in silence, words didn't fit what needed to be said.

Julie's eyes went to Dr. West. She mouthed the words "Thank you." Dr West smiled back at Julie and made her way out of the room.

***

Later That Night

After everyone left, Sam lay in the hospital bed, unable to sleep. The night pressed thick against the windows. A hum filled the air, electric but faint.

The dragon on her arm glowed softly, just for a second.

Sam sat upright, breath catching in her throat. Her reflection in the window seemed to blink half a second too late. A whisper, not from the room but from *inside*, brushed across her mind:

"It is not over. You are marked now."

She clutched her arm, feeling warmth, not pain, but something *awake.*

Sam rose from the hospital bed and stood in front of the window, staring out into rainy landscape of Chester. She looked at the darkened glass, her reflection staring back... but it wasn't alone.

Standing beside her in the window, faint but unmistakable, was Raincloud.

His weathered face bore a small, tired smile. Eyes kind. Proud.

Sam didn't move. Didn't breathe. She just watched as he gave her the smallest of nods... and then faded into the dark, like a mist at dawn.

Tears welled in her eyes, but she smiled too. Just a little.

She wasn't alone. Not really. Not anymore.

***

Fresno PD HQ

Detective Rogers sat at his desk, the familiar hum of the station filling the background. The room smelled faintly of burnt coffee and old carpet, comforting in a strange, weary way.

He flipped slowly through the case notes and photographs he'd copied from Kirby's files. He'd talked the old detective into letting him make duplicates before leaving Connecticut, claiming it was for reference. But Rogers knew better. These weren't going into any official reports, they were for him. For *his* files.

He reached into the bottom drawer of his desk and pulled out a worn manila folder. Inside were the notes and photos from cases he'd worked long ago, ones where Raincloud had helped him, often without credit, always without question. With care, he tucked the Connecticut folder in beside them.

Then he pulled out a small flat pouch, beaded, hand-stitched. Raincloud had given it to him back at the rest stop. Just a quiet handoff and a nod.

Rogers turned it over in his palm, shaking his head. "That one's for the ages," he muttered to himself. "I won't be forgetting it."

He rubbed the pouch gently, then slipped it back into his jacket pocket.

A light knock tapped at the office door.

The captain leaned in. "Well, the traveler returns. So Rogers, did you solve the cases here and there? Do we pin a medal on you now?"

He chuckled, leaning against the doorframe.

Rogers glanced up and gave him a wry look. "Turns out, while they looked alike, there wasn't anything solid in the retired detective's files. Just a bunch of similarities and dead ends. I guess both cases stay cold, Cap. Just like the ones back in Connecticut."

The captain sighed and crossed his arms. "That's too bad. I figured if anyone could crack 'em, it'd be you. Not like you to let a case go unsolved."

Rogers leaned back in his creaky wooden chair, the springs groaning beneath him. "Well, Cap, I guess the old saying holds true. Can't win 'em all."

The captain grinned. "Welcome back, Rogers. Hope you're rested. We've got a stack of fresh ones waiting."

Rogers gave a half-smile, but his eyes lingered on the manila folder beside him.

"I'm ready," he said. "Let's get to work."

Epilogue: The Living and the Marked

Two weeks later, Sam stood at the edge of the hill behind Raincloud's home, where the brush met the sky. A soft wind tugged at her jacket, the same one she'd worn that night. The earth was uneven beneath her boots, the grass brittle from early frost.

She held a small pouch in her hand, the last thing Raincloud ever gave her. Inside were a few remaining pinches of that ash. She didn't know if it still held power. Maybe it never did. Maybe it was all in the gesture.

"Still showing up early at your own ceremony," she murmured to the sky. "Guess you get to do that now, too." No reply came, but she wasn't expecting one.

Behind her, Dr. West approached slowly. Julie stood a little further off, watching with a cautious tenderness.

"You okay?" Dr. West asked, stepping to Sam's side. Sam nodded. "Closer than I've been in a long time."

They stood in silence.

"I remember everything now," Sam said. "What it did. What it tried to make me give up. The way it used people I loved...."

Dr. West put a gentle hand on her shoulder. "But it didn't take you. That matters."

Sam opened the pouch, sprinkling a pinch of ash into the wind. It caught the breeze and spiraled upward like smoke, like memory.

"I still hear it sometimes," she said, turning to Dr. West. "Not the shadow. The other one. Uktena. It's quieter now. But... it's in me. Watching."

Dr. West's expression didn't change. "You lived through something unimaginable. That doesn't leave you untouched."

"No," Sam said, "but it doesn't mean I'm broken."

Julie walked up behind Sam and Dr. West. Julie's arms were wrapped around herself. "You ready?"

Sam gave one last look into the wind. "Yeah. I think so."

As they walked down the hill together, Sam glanced at the window of Raincloud's old cabin one last time.

For just a moment, she thought she saw his reflection again, standing there in the glass. Weathered. Smiling.

But when she blinked, it was gone.

Still, her chest felt lighter.

Marked, yes. But not alone.

Never again.

***

Dragon Tattoos and Piercings Shop

A week after the ceremony, Sam sat back in the worn leather chair, the familiar buzz of the tattoo machine humming steadily in the quiet shop. The faint scent of antiseptic mixed with ink filled the air.

Julie worked with steady, practiced hands, carefully bringing Sam's drawing to life, the Uktena, jaws stretched wide in a silent roar, crimson eyes blazing like embers, and Sam's own face framed fiercely within its maw.

War paint streaked boldly across the figure's cheeks, echoing the marks Sam herself bore, a permanent reminder of the night she faced the beast and lived to tell the tale.

The needle's rhythm was almost meditative, each pass binding them closer, not as hunter and hunted, but as two intertwined forces sharing one body, their fates sealed together for as long as she would live.

Sam's breath slowed, a quiet peace settling over her as the ink soaked into her skin, a silent vow etched in flesh.

www.ingramcontent.com/pod-product-compliance
Lightning Source LLC
Chambersburg PA
CBHW020509020726
47493CB00001B/247